Pitlochry's
Secret War

Pitlochry's Secret War

A NOVEL

Robert O. Scott

Matador
9 Priory Business Park,
Wistow Road, Kibworth Beauchamp,
Leicestershire. LE8 0RX
Tel: 0116 279 2299
Email: books@troubador.co.uk
Web: www.troubador.co.uk/matador
Twitter: @matadorbooks

ISBN 978 1789016 406

British Library Cataloguing in Publication Data.
A catalogue record for this book is available from the British Library.

Printed and bound in Great Britain by 4edge Limited
Typeset in 14pt Aldine by Troubador Publishing Ltd, Leicester, UK

Matador is an imprint of Troubador Publishing Ltd

This book is dedicated to all those who helped defeat the Germans, Italians and Japanese in the Second World War.

About The Author

Robert Scott was born in Glasgow in 1927. He served in the R.A.F. just after the end of the Second World War. His love of climbing Scottish hills took him to the wildly beautiful landscape of Assynt. As a ghillie/gamekeeper he happily lived there for many years. After his wife's death he moved to Pitlochry, where for more than twenty years, he's enjoyed quiet contented retirement.

Acknowledgements

For detailed information about Pitlochry and district the author is indebted to Collin Liddell's excellent book:

   Pitlochry - Heritage of a Highland District

For information about the explosion of Japan's secret experimental atomic device, the author is indebted to the book: *Beyond the Bamboo Screen* by Tom McGowran, OBE.

1

'Oh damn!' Ian Gray exclaimed as the ringing of the telephone shattered the silence of his small office.

He was annoyed at being disturbed when busy at the tedious wartime task of sorting out and counting all the food ration coupons left by last week's hotel guests.

However there was no trace of this annoyance in his voice as he lifted the receiver and politely said, 'Good morning. The Glen Hotel. Ian Gray speaking.'

'Good morning, Ian. John here.'

'Oh, hello, John. What are you after this time? More salmon fishing on the River Tummel?'

John chuckled, 'I'm keen to fish your hotel's great beat again, but not today, I'm afraid. This is an official police call.'

'"An official police call" regarding what?' Ian asked. 'Hotel business or Home Guard duties?'

'A bit of both actually.'

'Sounds intriguing. Go ahead then. I'm all ears.'

'Aye, I know you are,' John laughed. 'The trouble is that you're not the only one who's "all ears". Aye, and all mouth as well. So I'll not say any more over the phone. "Careless Talk Costs Lives," you know.'

'Oh yes, I understand. I'm staring at a "Careless Talk" poster as I speak. It's on the office wall in front of me; it orders us to, *"Be Like Dad and Keep Mum".*'

Both these Second World War warning posters issued by the Ministry of Information vividly pictured the possible result of careless talk: A British merchant ship being sunk by a German U-boat.

There was no need for John to give the name of the other person who was "all ears".

Ian knew he was referring to "Auld Maggie", the venerable old-maid in almost tyrannical charge of Pitlochry's small manual telephone exchange tucked away behind the post office in a small lane off the main street of this neat wee North Perthshire town.

Not only did Auld Maggie listen in to all the most interesting calls that went through her exchange, but she often could not refrain from spreading eager gossip based on what she'd overheard. This habit of hers had been annoying in peacetime, in the depth of this wartime it could be much more serious.

Both men guessed she was listening in to their conversation, so when John said, 'I expect there's someone eavesdropping on us at present,' they were not surprised to hear a clicking sound that suggested that an annoyed Auld Maggie had taken the un-subtle hint and was no longer listening in.

But John – John Grant, the police inspector in charge of Pitlochry and North Perthshire – was taking no chances. He repeated, 'I won't say any more over the phone, Ian. Are you coming into Pitlochry today by any chance?'

'Aye, I'm going to the bank later this morning.'

John again chuckled, 'Do you need any police protection for your heavy bag o' swag?'

Ian returned his chuckles, 'No thank you, inspector. My bag of money isn't too heavy, not in these straitened wartime years. The biggest burden I'll carry are all the ration coupons I've to take to the damned bureaucrats at the local Ministry of Food office.'

'Well, Ian, if you call in at the police station about eleven I'll tell you all the secret 'gen' you need to know as both hotel owner and Home Guard commander. You might even get a mug o' char too.'

'I'll really appreciate a refreshing 'cuppa' after having sweated all the way on my auld bike.'

As Ian returned to sorting out the ration coupons for meat, sugar, tea etc. and placing them in neat piles before filling in the Ministry of Food forms – in duplicate- he wondered about the linked police, hotel, and Home Guard official business that could not be disclosed over the phone. He could not imagine what this 'hush-hush' information would turn out to be.

That the Home Guard were somehow involved made it especially intriguing for him as commander of the Pitlochry and district Home Guard. He was proud of the rank of major that went with this command.

He was also proud of all the part-time Home Guard soldiers under his control, especially as – like police inspector John Grant and himself – most of these willing, un-paid volunteers had fought in the First World War (many, again like John and himself, serving in Perthshire's famous regiment, The Black Watch) and were now, in this Second World War, getting on in years. Yet old age in no way diminished the keenness of these veterans.

Yes, Ian reflected, there had been good reason to feel pride in the brave patriotism of all these ageing men who, back in the grim days of 1940 when a German invasion of Britain seemed imminent, eagerly volunteered to do all they could to help the British Army repel these hated Hun invaders.

At that desperate time our Army in its battered, deeply apprehensive beleaguered state after its demoralising frantic withdrawal from defeated France was thankful for every offer of help it got.

How well Ian remembered that amazing time when, after the 'Phoney War' of winter 1939/40 when nothing much had happened, the German Army's Blitzkrieg thundered into action and in just over three months had invaded, defeated and occupied Denmark, Norway, Holland, Belgium and then, unbelievably, France.

It seemed that only the salty waters of the English Channel, with help from the Royal Navy and the R.A.F could prevent a successful invasion of Britain by the unstoppable German Army led by their invincible Panzer Divisions.

Ian had known that any Hun invaders would hardly land here in rural inland Perthshire. But there had been the real menace of – and many wild rumours about – ruthless German paratroopers (some disguised as nuns!) landing in even the most remote parts of Britain.

Now in late September, 1943 there was no longer any threat of a German invasion. There were instead large British and American armies in constant training in preparation for invading and liberating France then thrusting on into Germany. Many had hoped (and Stalin had demanded!) that this Allied invasion would happen this year. It hadn't. Surely it would happen next year, 1944.

Ian supposed that, having served their purpose and no longer being required, the Home Guard might soon be disbanded. Perhaps that's what he'd hear about at the police station later this morning.

2

After telling his wife that he was setting out for Pitlochry, Ian strode round to the garage at the back of their hotel. When he entered the garage he, as usual, cast a tender glance over his dark blue Rover saloon car that he'd last used in that fateful summer of 1940 when he'd received his final meagre ration of petrol. Since then this car rested, drained and empty, on solid wooden blocks that held its forlorn wheels clear of the floor.

Again as usual, Ian wondered how long it would be before this bloody long war was won and he'd get any amount of petrol and once more delight in feeling his grand auld car awaken to smooth purring, mile devouring post-war life.

With a half smothered sigh he stooped to the mundane task of fitting his cycle-clips to the bottoms of his grey flannel trousers. He settled the haversack on his back then wheeled the sturdy old Raleigh Roadster bicycle out of the garage.

From the hotel's pillared entrance he cycled out onto the minor side road that sloped up to meet the main A9 road that went through the heart of Pitlochry.

Again as usual he gave a rueful grin as he engaged his bike's uphill gear. Again he applied extra pressure to his labouring thigh and leg muscles. Was this increased effort now required an unmistakable sign of his advancing age? Or was this and all the other sloping roads and paths in this district mysteriously getting ever steeper?

He turned right and welcomed the ease of the main road's flatness. The war-imposed dearth of traffic added to the gentle pleasure of this easy cycling from his hotel at Pitlochry's northern outskirts to the centre of that small Perthshire town.

As he passed a row of neat grey houses Ian again noted how drab all their tiny front gardens were. Pre-war all these modest gardens had blazed a fine display of flowers. Roses of many flamboyant colours had been the delightful scentful heart of all that frivolous beauty. Now in these harsh wartime years only vegetables were grown there.

In every British garden it was the same, only patriotic vegetables and fruit were grown to help feed the drastically rationed nation and reduce the amount of food that had to be brought in by the U-boat menaced ships of our gallant, largely un-sung, Merchant Navy seamen heroes.

Ian's thoughts were distracted by the noise of an approaching train. As he cycled across the road bridge over the Perth to Inverness railway line he was engulfed in a cloud of black smoke. For him, as for all older veterans, that smoke's familiar acrid smell instantly reminded him of the troop-trains of the First World War that had taken the massed ranks of brave young British men to war and, for all too many, to hideous violent death.

Ian quickly cycled onwards.

Soon he saw a much more pleasant scene of smoke, steam and flames. A sight that always cheers: 'Big Tam', the massive local blacksmith sending sparks gaily flying as he hammered his mighty blows.

War's grim shortage of petrol had brought many British horses back to work in farms and forests. The shoeing needs of all these patriotic horses kept alive the farrier's ancient skills that had been in danger of dying out in many over-motorised districts.

'Big Tam' took quiet pride in his horseshoeing expertise. There were great demands for his services, but no matter how busy, he always found time to indulge in cheery blethers, un-malicious gossip and eager talk and passionate debate about all the latest war news. For many 'Auld Worthies' this blacksmith's workplace was a real haven: a grand masculine domain of iron, sweat, smoke and soot where for some gregarious camaraderie hours they could escape from their auld wife's nagging complaints about all the wartime shortages and their long weary hours of queuing for their rationed food.

Ian had spent many a pleasant winter hour enjoying the cosy glowing warmth of that place and of the blacksmith's ever cheery company. Today however he merely gave a friendly wave and cycled on his way.

He passed another row of neat grey houses whose front gardens were even smaller than the one's he'd already seen. Even these tiny suggestions of gardens strove to grow a few patriotic tatties and turnips.

He smiled as he saw another patriotic site: three flags hanging limply in the calm, mild, September air. They hung from the three flagpoles slanting out from the front of a small hotel. Like many rural hotels and country mansions this little Pitlochry hotel had been requisitioned for wartime use.

The largest central flag proudly displayed the bright red, white and blues of the British 'Union Jack'. No surprise to see that historic National Flag. However even those like Ian who knew why they were there it always seemed strange to see the other two foreign flags.

One displayed the colours of the Dutch National flag. The other, even more surprising, was the proud ensign of the Royal Netherlands Navy. It made a strange incongruous show as it flew here in Pitlochry as far away as it was possible to get in Scotland from the Atlantic Ocean and the North Sea.

The explanation for these two flags was simple: that small hotel was now a hostel, a haven of rest and recreation for officers of the Free Dutch Navy on a few days much needed leave.

When their country had been forced to surrender to the all-conquering German Army in 1940 these Dutch sailors had, with great skill and daring, evaded the searching German Navy and Luftwaffe and sailed their warships to Britain. Ever since then they had been engaged in helping the Royal Navy in its desperate never-ending struggle to defeat the German U-boats that were sinking all too many British merchant ships.

These brave Dutchmen, their homeland still occupied by the hated Huns, were thankful to get away for a short time as far as possible from the deadly Atlantic dangers to enjoy the sympathetic hospitality of the Scottish people.

Ian and his wife, Anne, organised dances for these very appreciative sailors. Some passionate romances and more than one whirlwind wartime marriage between Dutch sailors and young Scottish women had flamed to brilliant hectic life thanks to those dances.

As he cycled past these three flags Ian gave them a friendly informal salute.

So far on this familiar journey he had seen few pedestrians, but now, surrounded by Pitlochry's varied shops, he passed many. Most were housewives, shopping basket in one hand, purse and precious ration-books grasped in the other, all hurrying in eager anxious hope that some butcher or grocer might have some rare special treat on offer today to supplement their meagre official rations. Often they were disappointed.

But today, noticing the gossipy excitement of the queue of housewives overflowing from one butcher's shop, he guessed there was something special being got from "under the counter" there. Ian wished them success in their urgent quest: these women, many quite elderly, surely deserved an occasional culinary reward for all their patient queuing in all weathers.

They also deserved praise for all their skilful domestic "make doing and mending" in the midst of this war's all too many shortages and scarcities.

As he cycled by the bulk of the Fisher's Hotel that dominated this part of the road, Ian smiled at the thought that that large hotel was not now a real competitor to his own hotel. Many of the Fisher's bedrooms were full of Glasgow children, evacuees from the menace of the German Luftwaffe's deadly bombing.

Ian's gaze now switched to the other side of the road and to the Butter Memorial Fountain. The mellow September sunshine gave a pleasant silvery glitter to this imposing monument's white Aberdeen granite. Local opinions were divided about this structure. Some thought it most attractive and with its soaring spire and its many granite crosses a most fitting memorial to a gallant Victorian Christian Officer and Gentleman.

Others thought it like a vulgar sugary wedding cake, an ostentatious tribute to the wealth and power of the Landed Gentry.

Ian had ambivalent feelings about this monument's dominating glaring presence, but it did not disturb his aesthetic senses. His wife, Anne, being more artistic, more sensitive, called it 'That flamboyant Gothic Monster'. But even she had to admit that its drinking fountain with its fresh cool water was a much appreciated feature during mid-summer's sweaty heat.

When this monument had been built in 1887 in memory of Colonel Archibald Butter, the fact that it jutted out into Pitlochry's main road did not matter. There was little traffic then, and that horse-drawn traffic moved at a safe, slow, sedate plodding pace.

Things were different now. While the severe austerities of this Second World War had greatly reduced the amount of non-essential vehicles on Britain's roads there was a new danger: the large number of young, inexperienced, eager British Army drivers. These over-confident youthful soldiers were a bit of a danger in daylight hours; at night in the strictly enforced blackout, their army truck's headlights covered all over, except for a narrow slit of light to guide them, they were a real menace.

Now that the United States was – rather belatedly – in the war as our brave Ally, many young American soldier-drivers, unfamiliar with our confusing total blackout and the strangeness of driving on the 'wrong' side of the road, were an even greater menace. Fortunately not very many of them were stationed in Scotland. Most were based in Southern England and were preparing for the coming invasion and liberation of France.

The local council's roads department hoped that the broad band of white paint curving around the front of the jutting memorial would alert all nocturnal British and American army drivers to the danger of its looming presence. It had succeeded so far.

Ian free-wheeled a short distance down the road's gentle slope then stopped outside the requisitioned shop that was now the local office of the Ministry of Food. Before taking his hotel's food coupons into this bureaucratic stronghold he gazed across to the opposite side of the road where more white paint glowed its warning not only around, but actually on the lower part of the dainty, high spired round tower that was part of an historic building.

This old building also jutted out into the main road. It was also connected to the Butter family. Its history went much further back than the Victorian times of the Butter Memorial Fountain. It had been this family's ancestral Mansion House.

On the 3rd September, 1745 Prince Charles Edward Stuart (Bonnie Prince Charlie) was leading his ragged tartaned

Jacobite Army along General Wade's grand new military road that had been built for the use of Government soldiers, not by these savage Highland Rebels.

As the Prince and his army passed through the small hamlets that would soon amalgamate to become the village of 'Pitlochrie' the Prince was invited into the Butter Mansion for rest and refreshment. He gracefully accepted this hospitality.

Now, coming up for exactly two hundred years since then, this jutting, twin towered old mansion was still affectionately known as the 'Prince Charlie House'.

It was no longer a mansion; time had humbled it down to being two shops. One shop had done a lively trade with pre-war tourists looking for postcards of Ben Vrackie, The Falls of Tummel and other grand local views. (None of Blackpool's vulgar saucy seaside postcards had been sold in genteel Pitlochry). This shop was now closed for the duration of the war.

The other shop, snug between the two old round towers, was still in use. The pole slanting up with the red and white of blood and bandage coiling along it proclaimed this now to be a barbers.

Ian smiled as he remembered the many times he'd had his hair cut there. The barber was known as 'Limpy Jimmy': a severe war wound in his thigh had limped him out of the army in 1916. He'd received a miserable disability pension.

Always as Limpy Jimmy was plying the tools of his hairdressing trade he would also ply his captive customer with all the latest local news and whisper him the most shocking of the local gossip. 'Aye,' Ian happily mused, 'you can bet on getting something more than just a haircut at good auld Limpy Jimmy's.'

He now entered the much less cheerful Ministry of Food office to, complying with all the strict correct procedures, hand over his food ration coupons.

That dreary business finished, he cycled a short distance down the main road then turned into Bonnethill Road, that place where no one any longer made Pitlochry Bonnets.

His labouring legs complained and his breath gasped in sympathy as this road got steeper. Dismounting, he pushed his sturdy old bike up between and beyond the police station and Scotland's Hotel. He would go to the bank first, complete the pleasant task of paying in money, then come back down to keep his appointment with his friend, Inspector John Grant.

3

As Ian came out of the Bank of Scotland he almost bumped into a hurrying young lady.

He smiled a stammering apology, then, recognising her, exclaimed, 'Oh, hello Miss Kerr... Oh, I'm sorry, of course you're no longer Miss Kerr, are you? You are Mrs...? Mrs...? I'm afraid I've forgotten your new married Dutch name.'

'It's Mrs van Karson... Mrs Alice van Karson.' She beamed a charming blushing smile, 'It sounds fine, doesn't it?'

'Aye, it certainly does. Again I give you my hearty congratulations on your happy marriage.'

As Ian smiled and stared at Mrs. van Karson his masculine mind admired her trim attractive figure, her glorious blond hair and the way her whole being seemed aglow with the joy of married love's pure bliss.

His baser male instincts certainly found her well worth staring at. Almost ashamed, he quickly asked, 'How's your husband getting on?'

This was a subject Alice delighted to talk about. She gasped, 'Jan's been awarded the D.F.C (Distinguished Flying Cross) by the R.A.F you know!'

'Yes, I heard that. Congratulations. You must be real proud of him.'

With gleaming eyes and even brighter smiles Alice agreed, 'Oh yes, I am. Jan's a real hero!'

Ian thought of the random chances, the trials and tribulations of war that had brought that young Scotswoman and young Dutchman together.

Alice Kerr had been a primary schoolteacher in Glasgow. When war was declared on 3rd September, 1939 she helped other teachers usher their young pupils onto the special train that would take these excited innocent evacuees to the safety of Scotland's more remote countryside.

Such trains carrying thousands of young children were steaming out of every British city. Anxious parents and all others remaining in these rumour-rife cities prayed that at least these children would survive should what they feared soon come about: massive bombing by fat Herman Goering's formidable Luftwaffe.

While the threat from German high-explosive bombs was worry enough, a much greater dread was that – following the example of Mussolini's air force in Abyssinia and Japanese warplanes in China – deadly poison-gas bombs would be dropped. No one in Britain, civilians and the armed forces, went anywhere without their precious gas mask.

Alice's train stopped at Pitlochry and the neat small railway station became a bustle of excited apprehension as weary children were sorted out then taken to requisitioned hotels or their allocated private houses.

These young Glasgow evacuees and the two teachers soon settled into safe calm life in the tranquil beauty of North Perthshire. But even here they always carried their gas masks with them.

Squadron Leader Jan van Karson, D.FC. had been an officer in the Royal Netherlands Navy when Holland was defeated by the Germans in 1940. He escaped to Britain and, being an experienced pilot, was drafted to the new 320 Dutch Squadron that was being formed under the command of the R.A.F.

This squadron's patriotic Dutch airmen were eager to hit back at the hated Huns who were occupying their sad country.

So time after time Jan bravely flew bombing missions against German ships and other targets.

He was lucky – after 70 of these dangerous missions his plane had never been seriously damaged by any enemy ship's savage flack or by a Luftwaffe fighter's deadly fire. He and none of the three men crew of their twin-engined Mitchell bomber had been even slightly injured.

Then on his 71st mission his luck ran out.

A Messerschmitt's raking cannon fire had badly damaged his plane. He had been forced to 'ditch' it onto the cold North Sea.

But he and his crew survived even this savage ordeal unharmed. They had been quickly picked up from their dinghy by an R.A.F, Air-Sea Rescue launch that had been guided to them by their distress signals.

Having 'Ditched in the Drink' these four brave Dutchmen automatically became members of the R.A.F.'s exclusive Dolphin Club, membership of which was confined to those who'd had this experience.

They were issued with a Golden Dolphin Badge to pin beside their tunic's varied medal ribbons.

Jan and his crew were now transferred to R.A.F. Coastal Command and were trained to fly Britain's largest aircraft, the huge, four-engined Sunderland flying boat.

The Royal Navy's Battle of the Atlantic against German U-boats had started on the first day of the war. It had never ceased since then. It was a battle we had to win, for if we lost it we would lose the war as well. Now in 1943 it had reached a critical stage. Not only did Britain's vital war supplies need to arrive, but an entire United States Army had to be shipped across the U-boat haunted North Atlantic.

Not all American soldiers travelled in large, well-protected convoys. Some – up to ten thousand at a time – sailed in the huge British liners, the *Queen Mary* and the *Queen Elizabeth*. Even painted in their dull battleship grey these ships were a picture of graceful nautical beauty as they sped at full speed towards the Clyde Estuary and were met and protectively circled by Jan's and other Sunderland flying-boats, all heavily-laden with bombs and deadly depth charges.

Fanatical young Nazi U-boat captains drooled at the thought of sinking one of these gigantic troopships crammed with all those American soldiers.

How wonderful to be rewarded by being awarded the highest order of the Iron Cross. And, most wonderfully of all, receive that fabulous medal direct from the hands of the Glorious Führer!

Eventually what had been thought almost impossible was achieved: that entire United States Army crossed the North Atlantic without the loss of a single American soldier.

After having flown on many other convoy protecting missions, Jan and his augmented crew were credited with having sunk two U-boats and having damaged a third.

Jan was awarded a well-deserved D.F.C.

4

Standing outside Pitlochry's Bank of Scotland, Ian Gray, having duly admired it, returned the precious black and white photograph to Alice van Karson.

With real reluctance Alice put that wondrous photo back into her large handbag. She much preferred having that photo of her husband out in the open being shown to everyone she met.

Wasn't she entitled to proudly show that photo? There were not many young wives who, like her, had a picture of her husband standing outside bomb-damaged Buckingham Palace and modestly displaying the D.F.C. he'd been presented with by the King.

King George VI, unlike his abdicated older brother, tried to conscientiously carry out his many wartime duties despite his deep shyness and awkward stammer. On this occasion he'd even managed a stammering joke about the brave Dutch airman's real 'Dutch Courage'.

Ian smiled and, diverting Alice's thoughts from that special photo, asked, 'Have you reported in at the police station as usual this week, Mrs. van Karson?'

Bursting into sudden laughter, Alice exclaimed, 'No, I've not! I won't ever sign on there again. At last – at long last – I'm finished with all that damn bureaucratic nonsense, thank God!'

Ian's laughter merged with hers, 'That's great. I'm delighted to hear it. Yes, it really was ridiculous nonsense, wasn't it?'

They were referring to the fact that, although Miss Alice Kerr was of pure, proud Scottish blood and true to her working-class Glasgow roots, was passionately anti-fascist (In the Spanish Civil War her communist uncle had joined the International Brigade and fought against Franco's Fascists) yet when she changed her status from being a Scottish maid to being a Dutch officer's wife some British civil service bureaucrat had decreed that her new name, Mrs. van Karson, sounded suspiciously alien. She therefore had to sign on once per week at Pitlochry police station to let the local authorities see that she had not moved away, was not doing anything suspicious, was not really a Nazi spy.

Even though Alice's hero husband, his Dutch and British commanding officers and local police inspector John Grant all vouched for her excellent character and sincere patriotism still that obscure bureaucrat, puffed up with his own self-importance and "armed with his little, brief, authority" insisted that Mrs. van Karson. 'that Dutch alien', must continue signing on each week.

This nonsense continued for a full six months until now at last some higher, wiser Governmental power had intervened and ended this annoying senseless wartime farce.

With renewed laughter Alice continued, 'Not only will I never again sign on at Pitlochry's police station, but from next week I won't be anywhere near that damn place.'

'Oh why? Where will you be? Where are you going?'

With gasping eagerness and aglow with anticipatory happiness Alice explained, 'I'm going to Helensburgh. Jan and I are going to share a flat there when he's off duty. I'll work as a part-time teacher, but I'll always be there in our own wee flat when Jan returns from his long, exhausting and dangerous convoy protecting Atlantic patrols.'

'Jan will be based at Helensbrough too?'

'More or less. He's actually stationed at the large R.A.F. Coastal Command flying-boat base at Rhu, just outside Helensburgh.'

With sudden dramatic speed Alice's hand flew to silence her guilty mouth. 'Oh, I shouldn't be telling you all that, should I?'

'No, you shouldn't. You certainly shouldn't.' Ian grinned and quoted the official warning posters: '"Careless talk costs lives," you know.'

With her hand hovering over her mouth Alice smiled, 'Oh but surely I'm doing no harm telling you all this, am I? There's no fear of you being an enemy spy, is there?'

'No,' Ian laughed, 'I assure you I'm not a nasty Nazi spy!' He noted it was her left hand that hovered over her mouth. He also noted how well that quivering hand displayed her engagement and wedding rings. He thought, 'Oh, I better not be an old cynic and think that display of these rings is done deliberately. No, I'm sure there's no deep feminine guile there. Anyway wouldn't she be quite justified to show-off these golden symbols of her blissful married state. This state made all the more precious by the constant lurking fear of this dreadful war's threat of sudden violent death.'

Alice contritely said, 'Oh, I'll need to be sure to obey these posters and make no more "careless talk" when I'm living in Helensburgh, won't I?'

'Aye, you will. Helensburgh's on the Clyde Estuary, isn't it?'

'Yes, it is. I've had a few pleasant pre-war day trips to it from Glasgow. I'm really looking forward to living there.'

'And your hero husband living with you there will make it a real paradise, won't it?'

Her deep blushes confirmed this. To ease her embarrassed state Ian said, 'I remember seeing pre-war posters in Pitlochry's railway station that extolled the beauty of the Clyde Coast and urged everyone to take holidays there. These posters showed idyllic scenes of cloudless skies, charming hills and jaunty Clyde paddle-steamers gaily sailing over calm blue seas. They boldly declared the Clyde Coast to be "Scotland's Bracing Riviera!"'

'"The Bracing Riviera"?' Alice queried. She laughed, 'Often on rain-soaked holidays at Rothesay, Millport or Dunoon poor shivering Glasgow holiday makers have found that "Riviera" to be just too bracing.'

'Anyway I'm sure Jan and you will be very happy at Helensburgh whatever the weather. You'll come and visit us here sometimes, won't you?'

'Oh yes, of course we will. Jan and I will always have very fond memories of Pitlochry where we first met, and were married.

Merrily smiling Alice went into the bank.

Ian was about to mount his bicycle and freewheel down the slope of Bonnethill Road to the police station, but then he changed his mind.

Holding the bike he walked slowly down instead. This gave him time to adjust his mind from its cheery state after his pleasant meeting with Alice.

He still had a vivid mental picture of Glasgow's loud, cheery, hardy crowds going 'Doon the Water' to Scotland's bracing Riviera.

With an effort he forced that bright vision out of his mind and concentrated on having a more solemn face that suggested sadder thoughts.

He entered the police station and greeted Sergeant Ewan MacLeod with all due solemnity.

This tall white-haired elderly police sergeant had come out of retirement for the war years while many younger policemen were serving in the army. His broad, cheery ruddy face and his ready laughter plus the re-assuring strength of his sturdy presence had made him a popular 'well-kent' character in and around Pitlochry.

This had been true during his many years as the districts only police sergeant. He'd still been a happy popular character during his retirement. This held true when he returned to his patriotic wartime duties.

Held true until three months ago.

On a never-to-be-forgotten awful day he and his weeping wife received the message every British family lived in fear of receiving.

The grim faced telegraph boy – that 'small messenger of death' – had delivered the dreaded flimsy yellow telegram from the War Office informing them, with deep regret, that their son, Corporal Colin MacLeod, had been killed in action.

Colin was their only son.

This tragic news almost killed the dead soldier's Mother.

It did kill the Father's smiles and ready laughter.

5

'The inspector's expecting you, Ian,' Sergeant MacLeod said. He lifted the flap on the wooden counter and ushered him through, 'Go right on into his office.'

Ian Gray knocked then opened Inspector John Grant's office door.

The inspector smiled, 'Ah, good to see you, Ian.' He pointed at the chair at the other side of his desk, 'Take a pew. How are you this fine morning?'

'Och, I'm fine... I'm fine. Thank God I'm not like poor Ewan. He's lost some weight since his son's death, hasn't he?'

'Aye he has. Poor Ewan right enough. My sad subdued sergeant's nothing like the ready laughing happy character he used to be.'

'That's understandable of course.' Ian sighed, 'It could happen to any of us.'

Each man thought of his own son: one serving in the Royal Navy, the other in the Army.

Giving a sudden grin the inspector asked, 'Have you seen this morning's paper? There's great cheerful news in it.' He slid the Daily Express across his desk to Ian.

With delight Ian read the paper's bold triumphant headline: 'Italy Surrenders!'

'Yes, I heard this great news on the wireless.'

There was the additional encouraging news that the British and American Allied armies in Italy had made large-scale amphibious landings near Salerno. Surely the whole of Italy would soon be liberated and the fighting there cease? Or would it?

Although the Italians have given up the fight, the hard-pressed German army in Italy would surely tenaciously fight on. And some fanatic Nazi soldiers would surely turn on their cowardly former Italian Allies with savage fury.

Ian had a strong personal interest in all this. His son, Andy, was a 'Desert Rat' , a sergeant in the Black Watch regiment, part of the 51st Highland Division serving in Monty's 8th Army.

Andy had survived un-wounded through some three years of fighting in North Africa and then in Sicily. Might he now be one of the British soldiers fighting in Salerno?

Ian had secret solemn doubts about all the fighting in Italy ceasing soon. That seemed too much to hope far. From his experience of them in the First World War he knew what formidable fighters most German soldiers were, and in this even more terrible Second World War most young German soldiers with their indoctrinated Nazi beliefs and their oath of absolute loyal to their revered Führer were even more formidable than ever.

Ian folded the Daily Express and replaced it on the inspector's tidy desk. He admired the neat un-cluttered way John kept not only his desk but his entire office. Quite a contrast to his own untidy wee office in his hotel. He really should tidy it up before his tidy-minded wife nagged him about this once again.

His gaze now focussed on the two slim green files on John's desk. He strained to read the upside-down writing on these files.

John smiled at his straining effort then pushed both files across his desk. 'Here, Ian, take them. Read them.'

Stamped across each file in glaring slanting red was the word, 'Confidential'.

Ian grinned, 'Oh, only 'Confidential." Not "Top Secret" I'm disappointed, John.'

'Och there's nothing about toilet rolls in these files so they're not classified "Top Secret."'

The two old friends laughed together as they remembered the time in 1916 when for a short spell they'd worked at Army Intelligence in London.

One of the strangest of the many strange tasks their rather shambolic Secret Service unit had been given to try to sort out was the one concerning Top Secret toilet rolls.

The new Whitehall department, The Ministry of War Production, keen to increase its authority and power was probing into all other Government Departments to try to increase their efficiency and reduce their shameful squandering wastes. This task was urgent in that time of grim austerity and severe shortages brought about by German U-boats sinking all too many British merchant ships.

A power-giddy bureaucrat in this eager new department wanted to know why the Royal Navy staff in the Admiralty used many more Government issued toilet rolls than the Army did in the War Office.

In pursuit of this mystery many polite letters, less polite memos and quite nasty scribbled notes passed back and forth between these three Government Departments.

The bulk of this unique correspondence was kept in one thick, and ever getting thicker file classified as 'Top Secret'.

Eventually Winston Churchill, once more back in power, scrawled across this quaint file, 'This ridiculous lavatorial bumf must at once cease to circulate.' As he initialled this strict order surely Winston must have smiled. How very appropriate that his initials were 'W.C.'!

His orders were obeyed. That Top Secret file, tied up with red tape, was hidden away in the deepest, most secret vault of one of these departments. Probably it is still there mouldering away, still keeping its Top Secrets secret!

Ian opened the first slim, merely 'Confidential' file. He had seen it before. It contained details of one Pitlochry man: Professor William Osborne. There were a string of impressive academic letters after his name. They meant nothing to non-academic Ian.

A report from Glasgow Police's Special Branch revealed that this professor was a leading physicist engaged in very important, very secret, scientific war work for the British Government. His cutting-edge research was carried out at a secret establishment 'somewhere in England'.

The demanding urgency of his work allowed the professor very little leisure time. On his all too rare few days leave he always headed for his chalet home in Pitlochry and, hopefully, for some relaxing, war-forgetting salmon fishing on Ian's hotel beat of the River Tummel.

On each of these refreshing short holidays the professor, as instructed, informed Inspector Grant that he was back in Pitlochry for a few days. The inspector, also obeying instructions, informed Ian of this and between the police and Home Guard provided unobtrusive protection for this V.I.P.

This Special Branch report instructed the inspector that if any stranger arrived and seemed to take an unusual interest in Professor Osborne that suspicious person should be questioned, detained if thought necessary, and Special Branch informed at once.

This clandestine protection of the professor when in his large comfortable chalet home was made quite easy for the

Pitlochry Home Guard as their base was virtually right beside that chalet.

These Home Guard headquarters were the Territorial Army armoury and drill hall. With all the young soldiers now being in the 'Real Army' this large building was used mainly by the Home Guard, Army Cadets and Boy Scouts.

On every professor-guarding occasion to date nothing in the least interesting had happened. No suspicious stranger had appeared. No mysterious lurking danger had materialised out of the darkness of the strictly blacked-out Perthshire countryside.

Some of the oldest and keenest of the Home Guard's many keen old-timers, veterans of more than one war, after enduring many weary hours of boring, semi-hidden sentry duty almost wished for some action. Something to alert their semi-dormant senses and send welcome alarm signals tingling through their sleepy old nerves.

Rather disappointed, Ian closed that familiar 'Confidential' file. Nothing new there. So why was his friend, Inspector Grant, showing him it again?

Sensing his disappointment, John Grant smiled, 'I think you'll find the other file much more interesting, Ian.'

He did. He had never seen this second 'Confidential' file before. Like the first one it was all about just one man. A quite different man. Someone Ian thought he knew fairly well. Would this second Special Branch confidential report change his mind about him?

6

The man named in the Special Branch report was the Irish chef Ian had been employing at his hotel for the last three months: Daniel Bailey.

Being from the Republic of Ireland, that independent country which was wisely keeping out of this terrible war, Daniel was free from Britain's draconian wartime rules and regulations.

There was no conscription in the Republic, instead there were thousands of Irish volunteers who were soldiers in the British Army. Many were serving with courage and distinction. From the report Ian saw that two of Daniel's brothers must be doing just that. Both had been promoted to sergeants and one had been awarded the Military Medal for outstanding bravery during the savage fighting at the British victory at El Alamein.

A third brother worked in a Dublin bank, as did their father. Daniel himself had trained as a chef in a large Dublin hotel.

It seemed this Irish family must be fairly friendly towards the British. This must be the conclusion the British Police's Special Branch had come to when they discovered no reason to refuse Daniel's application to work in wartime Scotland.

Daniel had given varied reasons for wanting to work here. He wished to get out of the city and live in the countryside. He wanted to see other countries and other people. He thought it would be interesting to learn how a chef managed to cope with Britain's wartime food shortages and strict rationing. He was keen to get some trout and salmon fishing in his free time, as Ian had promised him he would if he worked at his Pitlochry hotel.

When the old widow who'd been cook at the Glen Hotel for most of his parents' time and then for much of Ian's own time had been forced to retire due to crippling arthritis his wife, Anne, had taken on the role of cook. But her increasing illness had now forced her to give up this demanding work and agree to them trying to get a new cook or chef to take over.

Like so much else in this fourth year of this seeming endless war reliable chefs and good cooks were very hard to find and keep.

So although they had some doubts about employing this unknown chef from Dublin, Anne and he decided they must give him a chance to prove his worth and help them out for at least the summer and autumn months when, despite the war, their hotel was usually quite busy, was even sometimes completely full.

Many of these hotel guests were army and navy officers on leave with their wives. Some were keen fishers hoping to catch salmon on the hotel's pools on the River Tummel.

All these soldiers and sailors greatly enjoyed the tranquillity of the Perthshire countryside, of being for a short time far removed from the sounds, dangers and horrors of war.

Some of the older, more senior Royal Navy officers were real bigoted blimpish characters. Having heard a few of those mostly English old diehards express disgust at the Irish Republic remaining neutral in this war and declaring that the entire Irish Island should still be part of the United Kingdom, still part of the Great British Empire, Ian was careful not to disclose to them that the chef who cooked their meals was an Irishman from Dublin.

Of course Daniel Bailey's kitchen domain was not a place these 'brass-hat' officers frequented or even thought about as long as their well cooked food arrived on time at their dining table.

If Daniel had any anti-English feelings about these blimpish officers and their demanding, shrill voiced snobbish wives whom he did not come into direct contact with but heard all about from the hotel staff who did, he kept these feelings to himself.

These female staff whispered complaints that this Irishman kept all his feelings and his thoughts about the war just too much to himself. He showed no emotions and expressed no strong opinions about the war's progress. They further complained that the only time he displayed eager animation was when he was talking about, what to them, was the boring subject of fishing.

At the end of the Special Branch Report there were orders that Ian was to keep an alert, but unobtrusive eye on Daniel Bailey and immediately report to Inspector Grant if he noted anything in the least suspicious about that Irish chef. The inspector in turn must report these suspicions to Glasgow Special Branch as a matter of real urgency, especially if that Irishman took any unusual interest in when Professor Osborne might be in Pitlochry and what he habitually did when he was here.

'Well, what do you make of that report?' John Grant asked as Ian closed the file and placed it on the inspector's desk.

Ian took a thoughtful pause before replying, 'First of all surely these two reports make it obvious that Professor Osborne must be a really important scientist. He must be engaged in vital war-work or Special Branch wouldn't be so concerned about his safety, would they?'

'Aye, I agree. He must be a real top-notch 'Boffin'. But what about Daniel Bailey? You ken him better than me. Now that you know more of his family background, his two brothers being brave volunteers in the British Army etc, does that influence your thoughts about him?'

'Och, although I'm much more in touch with him than you are, John, I hardly know him any more than you do. You liked him when you met him fishing at the river with me, didn't you?'

'Aye, I did. I was impressed by his effortless skill at casting with his long, double-handed fly-rod. And the Irish pattern salmon files he'd made himself were also most impressive.' John grinned, 'But his braw Irish flies weren't nearby as good at catching our Tummel salmon as our own reliable auld Scots flies were.

'Och I liked him fine as a real keen and skilled salmon fisherman, but what's he like when not fishing but working in your hotel?'

'Oh he's a good enough chef. He's fine with fairly plain basic dishes. He doesn't like anything too fancy, which is just as well in these grim times of wartime austerity. He's a reliable worker, good at getting on with things by himself in the hotel's kitchen.'

'Does he get on all right with the other hotel staff?'

'Oh aye, they all get along quite well together, although some female kitchen staff think he's just a bit too reserved. They find this most unusual for an Irishman.'

'You told me some time ago that your wife didn't care for him very much, Ian. Does that still hold true?'

'Oh yes it does,' Ian said. 'Anne can't give any rational reason for her dislike of Daniel, apart of course from the fact of him being from a neutral country and not being liable to be called-up for the army as her son had been.

Such a feeling is quite understandable, is quite a logical maternal feeling, but Anne admits she's also motivated by much deeper, more obscure feminine feelings that even she can't understand. Yes, John, her illogical feminine dislike of him remains almost as strong as ever.'

For some long moments the two men fell thoughtfully silent. With something like awe they stared into one another's questioning eyes as they tried to rationally understand that illogical thing: the female of the species amazing powers of intuition.

Both men were married long enough to be aware of the inexplicable reality of the irrational answers found by feminine intuitions and insights that almost always turned out to be more true and accurate than any answers suggested by mere male's pale and shallow logic.

These silent thoughts were ended by a muffled knocking on the office door.

'Oh, that'll be Ewan with our tea', John said.

Ian sprang to his feet and opened the door for police sergeant Ewan MacLeod who carried a tray laden with two large mugs of tea and a saucer containing two digestive biscuits. 'I'm sorry but there's only a wee touch o' sugar in both mugs today. Will that be all right?'

'Och yes, of course that'll be fine,' John said. 'And those biscuits are real braw too. You look after my guests and me really well, Ewan. Thank you. Why don't you bring your own char in here and share this tea-break with us?'

'Och, no thank you, inspector, not today." The sergeant forced something like a grin on his broad, sorrow-lined face, 'I'd better get back tae the front office. Someone has tae look after the "shop", ye ken.'

Once the door was closed and the steady thump of the sergeant's size twelve boots was heard retreating down the corridor John said, 'Poor Ewan, he puts a brave face on his misery over the death of his son, Colin.'

'Yes, it must be terrible to lose your only son. It must be a real desperate effort to keep up a brave, stoic outward appearance when your heart is full of misery. It's about three months since Colin was killed, isn't it?'

'Aye, just three months, so his death is still a fresh raw bleeding wound. But his poor parents hadn't seen Colin for more than two years before then as he'd been serving in the Middle East and then in India. Then he'd been killed by the bloody Japs when fighting with our poor "Forgotten Army" in the hellish jungles of Burma.'

After a solemn thoughtful silence Ian asked, 'How is Ewan's wife coping with the death of her son?'

'Och, not very well. She's devastated. Fortunately her daughter, Jeanie, has come home to stay with her parents and try to help them through this terrible time. Ewan tells me in confidence that it's not been easy. Her very special only son was always the mother's favourite child, the real apple of her eye. Her daughter always come second.'

Again there was a silent solemn pause as each man thought of his own only son, one serving in the Army, one in the Royal Navy. Both sons in constant danger. Both at risk of sudden death. How would each father cope with their son's death?

By themselves over late night drinks Ian and John had once frankly discussed these grim wartime worries that plagued many a sleepless night and brought hidden unease to many a quiet daylight hour.

Both men agreed that their own deep paternal grief over their son's death would be overshadowed by the deeper keener maternal grief of their wives. These old friends hoped that if they were ever faced with this terrible test they would somehow find the strength to help their wives through the darkest time.

Ian and John had agreed that in some ways the paternal and husbandly worrying of this Second World War felt at times more trying and stressful than many of the worries and deadly trials they had faced, and overcome, in the mud, blood and madness of the First World War.

Of course they had been much younger and fitter in their first war; had not been married, had not been fathers (not as far as they knew: there had been some unseemly frantic matings when a hideous Flanders death seemed all they had to look forward to).

Then John had given a sudden grin, 'Och, perhaps our dear wives will surprise us. Perhaps they'll conjure up hidden stoic strengths. Perhaps they'll do a Lady MacRobert on us.'

'Aye,' John had laughed, 'they might well do that. Lady MacRobert must be a real resolute character. You've met her haven't you, John?'

'Aye, I have. Aye, she's really quite a character. I've met her twice at Garth House. On both occasions she was most friendly, quite charming in fact. And that despite the tragic losses she'd suffered.'

Both men thought of the story of Her Ladyship and her unique reply to the Germans who had killed two of her brave airmen sons.

7

Garth House was Lady MacRobert's impressive Victorian-style shooting lodge set in her estate near Fortingall in North Perthshire.

'Aye, she was really quite charming when I met her there,' John repeated, 'but I knew that hidden behind that charm was a resolute strength that made her a formidable enemy when crossed. And the Germans certainly crossed her when they killed two of her brave sons.'

Actually three of her sons had been killed in the R.A.F. One had died in a plane crash before the war. The other two brothers had been shot down by the hated German enemy.

After the death of her third son Lady Robert's reaction was as that of every grieving mother. But soon, realising the useless wastefulness of a prolonged overflow of scalding tears, she resolved to channel her grief into something more practical, something that would hit back at the horrid Huns and to some degree avenge the death of her two gallant sons.

At first the Air Ministry were rather nonplussed by her Ladyship's unique request – or perhaps more a demand – that she pay for a new R.A.F. bomber to be built and named in memory of her dead pilot sons.

However her cheque for £25,000 was accepted by an Air Chief Marshall then quickly passed on to the watchful greedy Treasury.

Then in 1942 her very own, very special Stirling four-engined heavy bomber was built.

Her Ladyship alertly looked on to ensure that what she'd stipulated must be painted on the nose of 'her' bomber was correctly done.

It was. As the MacRobert's were a sept of the Robertson Clan it was that clan's coat-of-arms that, correct in every detail, was proudly emblazoned on 'her' huge Stirling aircraft. The clan's motto, 'Glory is the reward of Valour', became in effect, her Ladyship's gallant battle-cry.

Then in large letters was painted the bold statement that this Stirling bomber was *MacRobert's Reply*.

Heavy laden with many bombs this aircraft became Lady MacRobert's avenging angel bringing her defiant reply of death and destruction to the vile Germans who had spread their Nazi evil all over Europe.

For a time this story was little more than a local Perthshire legend, then somehow Winston Churchill heard of it.

Moved by this story of the death of her brave sons and wholeheartedly approving of her defiant reply, the Prime Minister ordered the Ministry of Information and the B.B.C. to tell this inspiring story to our undefeatable British Nation, our Empire, and especially to our new, our belated, American Allies in our desperate fight against Hitler's all too formidable armed forces.

Patriotic British propaganda made Lady MacRobert a national Hero. This story of Noble British Motherhood overcoming its deepest grief was on everyone's lips. But for many other grieving British Mothers that was a story they heard of with uncomprehending awe and wonder.

'Aye, she is a real outstanding character,' John again said. 'A real modern Boadicea!'

'Yes,' Ian agreed,' it was brave of her to overcome her grief in such a unique way.'

'I wonder if our son was killed would Betty fight back in such a brave way,' John asked. He then grinned, 'Although if our poor Jamie went down with his ship I doot Betty and me couldn't afford to buy a replacement Royal Navy warship as our "Grant's Reply".'

Joining in this dark humour Ian smiled, 'Och well if our Andy was killed and him only being an infantry sergeant in the Black Watch at least Anne and I could afford to buy a replacement rifle as our "Gray's Reply".'

John felt a sudden quiver of unease: might such talk be tempting fate? 'Och, Ian, that's enough of this foolish black humour. We better never let our wives hear us talk like that.'

'No, of course not.'

As both men had eaten their biscuits and drank their tea it was time for Ian to go. Before he did the police inspector repeated his instructions, 'Just try to keep a discreet eye on your Irish chef, Daniel Bailey. Do nothing to make him suspect that you're taking an undue interest in him. Be sure to let me know at once if you discover anything suspicious, anything I should inform Special Branch about.'

'Oh of course I'll keep an eye on him, but I think he might well be completely innocent.'

'That's as may be. I'll let you know whenever Professor Osborne is going to be staying in Pitlochry.'

'Yes, and as usual I'll tell Auld Sandy Robertson to keep the professor under unobtrusive protective watch while he's in his chalet home.'

Sandy Robertson was a corporal in the local Home Guard. For almost forty years he'd been a soldier in the Black Watch. He'd come through the Boer War and the First World War unscathed.

Keen to do his bit in this Second World War, he was happy to think that by discretely guarding this important professor he was helping Britain's war effort. There was little else he could do in this peaceful rural Perthshire countryside that seemed far removed from the horrors of this ongoing war.

Proud of his old regiment and well versed in its history, Auld Sandy thought of his protective watching as a contribution of this history.

The Black Watch's original duty had been to keep watch over lowland Perthshire and guard that lush farmland from wild, cattle stealing Highlanders sneaking down from the untamed wilderness's to the West and North.

Sandy often wondered just what obscure danger he was guarding his important professor from. Perhaps German Paratroopers were the only likely threat.

His guarding duties were made much easier by him being the caretaker of, and living in the house attached to Pitlochry's Territorial Army's drill hall and armoury, which was also the local Home Guard Headquarters and was conveniently situated only a short distance from Professor Osborne's chalet.

Sometimes before going on a lonely midnight watch around the professor's blacked out chalet Sandy fortified himself with a very rare, very precious warming dram. His memory then stimulated he fondly remembered the happy years when he was clad not in the Home Guard's dull khaki but in an army piper's bright red kilt. How smartly he used to stride out, young, keen, peacock proud, all aglow in the camaraderie glory of the Black Watch's grand pipe band.

Now, with the passing of so many years, his wheezy cigarette breath, his aching creaky knees, he only donned his bright auld kilt and tuned his pipes when called upon to play a lament over the open grave of yet another departed old friend.

As Ian was leaving the police inspector's office he said, 'Of course I'll say nothing to grand old Sandy, but I sometimes wonder if that professor really is so important as to deserve a guard – even if only mainly an old, semi-geriatric Home Guard one.'

'Yes, I've wondered that myself. It would be interesting to know what kind of secret scientific work he's engaged in, wouldn't it?'

'Aye, it certainly would. But I suppose, what with all the warnings about 'Careless Talk" and all that, he will never tell us and we might never get to know.'

8

As Ian free-wheeled down the gentle slope of Bonnethill Road he saw a traffic-jam on Pitlochry's main A9 thoroughfare.

Two convoys of army lorries, one going North, one South, had met, might even have collided at that jutting old obstacle, 'Prince Charlie House.'

There were four lorries in the North-bound convoy, there seemed more in the South-bound one. Every lorry was clad in a uniform of drab mud-brown paint or a camouflage confusion of browns and greens. All were now motionless and silent. The crowd of army drivers gathered around all this confusion were neither silent, nor still.

It was no surprise to hear agitated English and Scottish voices, but Ian was surprised to hear what sounded like German voices. Germans here in Pitlochry in 1943? Then he thought – surely they must be recently captured German soldiers on their way to the Prisoner of War camp near Bruar.

As Ian dismounted from his bike he saw a solitary figure standing in front of Pitlochry's war memorial. This man was not a German for he was clad not in a Nazi soldiers field-grey, but in familiar British Army khaki. But when in answer to Ian's friendly greeting this man replied it was clear he was not British.

As he quickly made clear he was a German-hating Pole in one of Britain's most brave Allies, the Free Polish Army. And as he indignantly declared, his proud Polish voice sounded nothing like the ugly guttural noises the bastard arrogant Huns made!

'You speak good English,' Ian said. He laughed, 'And you've picked up at least one British swear word.'

The Polish soldier also laughed, 'Oh I know more good bad English swear words.

I not say them to you. You am officer, no?'

'Well I was a major in the last war. I'm still a major, but only in the Home Guard.'

Springing to attention the Pole clicked his heels together and gave a smart salute.

'Oh you shouldn't salute me, not when I'm in civvies.'

There were now formal introductions: 'I am Corporal Sikorski, of the great, the brave, Free Polish Army.'

'I'm Major Gray of Pitlochry's gallant auld Home Guard.'

As they shook hands Ian said, 'The name Sikorski is familiar. Are you related to General Sikorski, the commander of your Free Polish Army?'

'No, I am no relation. I am always asked. Is annoying.'

He burst into loud laughter, 'A Scottish sergeant-major in your army called me not Sikorski, but "Corporal Fuckofski." He say is best name for me!'

Ian laughed and said, 'Well no matter what you're called you and all your free Polish soldiers do a great job of fighting the bloody Germans. My son had some Poles fighting beside him in Italy and he said they were really most tough and brave soldiers.'

This was true not only of these Polish soldiers but also of the free Polish pilots who had so aggressively flown their Spitfires against the formidable might of the Luftwaffe and helped the R.A.F. win the Battle of Britain in 1940.

These fearless Polish pilots felt that every Hun Heinkel and Junker bomber they shot down helped avenge the death and destruction these same planes had inflicted on Warsaw.

The Pole offered Ian an army-issue cigarette. While they were lighting-up the voices from around the motionless lorries further up the road increased in volume.

'They seem to be having trouble sorting out that traffic-jam up there. Shouldn't you be helping them?' Ian asked.

'Oh no. I only corporal. I leave that to officers and sergeants. I like peace or quiet here.'

'Peace and quiet,' Ian gently corrected.

'Peace and quiet, yes. Oh when will Poland – my poor Poland – ever get peace and quiet again?'

With compassionate empathy Ian tried to reassure the Pole. 'Oh I'm sure Stalin's victorious Red Army will soon kick Hitler out of Poland.'

'Oh yes, is true. Stalin will kick bastard Hitler out of Poland. But who then kick bastard Stalin out of poor Poland?'

Neither man knew it, but this was one of the many worries that tormented Winston Churchill when he tried to plan ahead and see the shape of post-war Europe.

On his darkest 'Black Dog' days he all too clearly remembered the disaster of the last war's amphibious Dardanelles campaign which, correctly or wrongly, he was blamed for.

Then there was this war's disastrous Combined Operations large scale raid and practice invasion at Dieppe in 1942.

What if the planned British and American invasion of Germany-occupied and strongly fortified France in May or June next year (1944) was also to result in disastrous failure?

This meticulously planned amphibious operation would be truly huge. Some 150,000 British, American and Canadian soldiers were to be landed on Normandy beaches on the first day (D/Day). There would be an invasion fleet 0f 5,300 ships and about 12,000 supporting aircraft.

Never before had there been a amphibious operation on the scale of this 'Operation Overlord.' If it was to fail the scale of the disaster would be equally gigantic.

Its failure would leave the way clear for Stalin's vast Red Army to thunder through not only Poland and all Eastern Europe but also through a defeated devastated Germany. And would a power-mad triumphant Stalin halt there? Might Western Europe also be overrun by his unstoppable Red Army?

Yes, Churchill thought in his despondent mood, he might live to see Europe's vile Nazi tyranny replaced by an equally vile Soviet tyranny. Oh in case next year's 'Overlord' invasion does fail we must pray that our scientific 'boffins' successfully develop their top secret atomic device in time.

After lighting another cigar and sipping another whisky, Winston gave an almost boyish mischievous grin, 'Yes, it will be damned grand to have that atomic ace up my sleeve the next time I deal face to face with that devious old rascal "Uncle Joe" Stalin.'

A gesturing and shouting Polish sergeant came hurrying down the road towards them. There was a loud exchange in Polish. Corporal Sikorski translated, 'All sorted out. All British and Polish soldiers all friends now. We all go now,' He held out his hand. Ian shook it, 'Good luck and good luck to your poor Poland.'

It seemed that a British and a Polish army lorry had met between these two traffic-hazards, Colonel Butter's memorial fountain and the historic "Prince Charlie House". They had merely scraped against one another and the only damage suffered was the loss of their jutting rear-view mirrors. All agreed it could have been much worse.

As Ian waved the last army lorry on its way he wondered how long these two traffic-hazards would be allowed to remain. Would the influential Butter family object to them being demolished? Or might they approve?

As he stood alone by Pitlochry's war memorial Ian welcomed the peaceful silence after all the 'sound and fury' of that minor traffic-jam.

His gaze was once again drawn to all those names neatly listed on that large granite cross. All those young men (some under the age of twenty) now lying at their eternal rest. And all those terrible deaths somehow being "To the Glory of God," as was claimed at the top of that cross!

Each of these 81 names was a tragic loss to mothers and wives. How many more names would this second, this even more terrible, even more widespread World War add to that long sad list?

He knew of only five local men's names including police sergeant Ewan Macleod's only son, Colin that would be added after this long war was finally won... if it was won! Sometimes it seemed it would never be done!

With understandable selfishness Ian hoped that his own son's name would not be added to this sad cross. And what about his two daughters? One was a W.A.A.F. (Woman's Auxiliary Air Force), one a nurse. While willingly doing their duty, they were in much less danger, were not fighting in the front line, were not serving in warships, were not fighter or bomber pilots.

Ian suddenly remembered that one name on the First World War list that was not of a young man, but of a woman. A young woman? He did not know. In her solitary place of honour was written: Staff Nurse MacBeth, QAIMNS (Queen Alexandria Nursing Service).

Once more Ian wondered how that nurse had died? From his own experience of the First World War he knew that many brave nurses volunteered to serve in Army Forward Field Hospitals that were not all that far behind the front lines and were only just beyond the range of German artillery.

Many wounded British soldiers owed their lives to the speed they were taken to, and the dedicated skilled attention they received from doctors and nurses at these Forward Hospitals.

Although out of range of German guns, those tented hospitals were well within range of Hun aircraft that, in a foretaste of things to come in the next World War, were dropping bombs on British Army bases behind the front lines and, despite the large red crosses on their roofs, sometimes on Forward Hospitals too.

Ian wondered if that was how Pitlochry's brave nurse MacBeth had died?

Then he again thought of his own daughters. Back in the grim year of 1940 when beleaguered Britain faced the threat of German invasion these two daughters had faced death from the bombing and strafing Luftwaffe.

To save giving their parents extra worry both daughters kept secret the fact that at that time they actually were in the front line!

Yes, their daughter, Jane, a corporal in the W.A.A.F, truly was in Britain's modern front line: its chain of secret radar stations set along England's South coast. Installed only just in time, these "all seeing eyes" guided Fighter Command's Spitfires and Hurricanes to approaching armadas of German planes. Operated by volunteer W.A.A.F's this new secret weapon was playing a vital part in helping the R.A.F. fight the Battle of Britain.

The Germans sent their most deadly, most dreaded and hated plane, the Stuka dive-bomber, to bomb and strafe those radar stations.

Diving almost vertically, its engine roaring, its siren wailing its mad, nerve-wracking banshee sound, that plane and its bombs were aimed straight at you. That Stuka was a truly terrifying sight.

And yet, despite all their best (or worst) efforts, these deadly planes failed to put many radar stations out of action for long. Killed and wounded W.A.A.F. radar operators were soon replaced by other brave W.A.A.F. and R.A.F volunteers. Damaged radar masts were soon repaired.

Corporal Jane Gray's radar site had been slightly damaged. The screen of her radar set was a blizzard of flickering snow. A civilian radar expert arrived. With what seemed magical speed he got her set working perfectly.

Hearing Jane's Scottish accent he smiled and asked, 'What part of Scotland are you from?'

'I'm from Pitlochry in Perthshire. Do you know it?'

'Yes, I know it well. I've had many happy holidays there. In fact my wife and I hope to retire there after the war.' He too had a pleasant Scottish voice. Before he could say more another civilian entered and said, 'Oh, there you are, Professor Watt. I wonder if you can help me. I can't get that other set going.' Both men then left.

Only later did Jane discover that that Professor was in fact the 'Father' of British Radar. He had got the Air Ministry to install his new-fangled radar just in time.

In 1942 his unique wartime services were recognised by him being awarded a knighthood. He then hyphenated his name and became: Professor Sir Robert Watson-Watt. After the war his wife and he did retire to Pitlochry.

Ian's other daughter, Mary, was a nurse. She too had been in the thick of things in that fateful year, 1940. She had served in a large London hospital during the worst of the Luftwaffe's Blitz.

Although quite far from London docks and the East End where most bombs were dropped, her hospital had a few bombs fall near it. Despite many shattered windows and clouds of ceiling plaster dust the unflappable surgeons, doctors and nurses continued to operate as normal as they attended to the endless stream of civilian casualties.

9

But now in September, 1943 things were quite different.

Jane Gray was serving at an R.A.F. airfield 'somewhere in Norfolk.' From there and all the other airbases in Eastern England R.A.F. Lancaster bombers and American Flying Fortress's were taking the war to Germany. They were giving Hamburg, Berlin, Dusseldorf and Essen a taste of what the Luftwaffe had inflicted on Warsaw, Rotterdam, London and Clydebank.

Now Lady MacRobert was not the only one making her defiant 'reply' loudly and clearly heard by the Germans.

In this same autumn Mary Gray was serving much closer to her Pitlochry home. She was nursing in what before the war had been Scotland's newest, largest, most luxurious rural hotel. Now this imposing Gleneagles Hotel was no longer a mecca for the pampered wealth. It was one of Scotland's largest military hospitals. It might be one of the largest, but it was not one of the busiest. Mary and the other nurses were surprised at how few ill or wounded soldiers were patients here, and yet extra wards were being prepared, more and more new beds being crowded into all those patient-less wards.

These puzzled nurses did not know it then but all over rural Britain similar activities were going on. The Army had requisitioned many stately manors, large country houses and hotels which were then converted into military hospitals. Yet every one of these hospitals had hardly any soldier patients.

Once they did get to know of all this countryside activity these nurses felt shivers of apprehension as they saw these rows of neat, spotless white-sheeted empty beds all waiting to be filled. They correctly guessed that all those empty beds were one part of the huge preparations for next year's allied invasion of German-occupied France. Those compassionate nurses tried not to dwell too much on nightmare thoughts of how many wounded, maimed or dying soldiers they would have to nurse after that huge invasion. They pictured those brave allied soldiers fighting out from French beaches and trying to liberate all France, Belgium and Holland. Then they would have to cross the Rhine and smash into Germany. And all this against fierce German resistance.

Little wonder that high-ranking army planners had ordered all those empty beds to be held ready waiting for the time when the flow of thousands of wounded allied soldiers might turn into a flood of tens of thousands. Although understandably anxious, those dedicated nurses knew they would rise to that chilling challenge. (As they most gallantly did!)

'Yes', Ian thought as he stared at that memorial to the First World War's dead, 'both my daughters are doing their bit in their long and bloody all-out war. I only hope to God that neither of their names will be on a Second World War addition to that grimlong list.'

His concern for his daughters was overshadowed by his constant deeper concern for his only son, Andy.

Having survived unharmed through two years of savage fighting as a 'Desert Rat' in North Africa and then through the amphibious landing at Sicily then Italy, Sergeant Andy Gray was still in the thick of the fighting as his 51st Highland Division fought its way up the length of Italy.

Remembering his own dark forebodings as, unscathed, he neared the end of that last World War, Ian's sensitive empathy put him in direct touch with what his son and his son's veteran comrades (young in years, old in experience of war) must be feeling... that unspoken dread that, having come through so much unharmed, their great good luck would end and Death would claim them just before this bloody long Second World War finally ended.

Ian groaned an apprehensive sigh then forced himself into a more cheerful mood as he mounted his eager waiting auld steed – his sturdy Raleigh Roadster bicycle.

Soon he was taking gentle pleasure in cycling this familiar route. As he swung out past the jutting round tower of 'Prince Charlie House' he imagined what a startling shock this unexpected hazard must be to Army drivers journeying North at night in this war's strictly enforced blacked-out dark. Little wonder that one army lorry had only just scraped past and left traces of its camouflage paint despoiling the tower's white painted purity.

Ian cycled un-swerving past that other hazard, the jutting Butter Memorial Fountain which stood in its innocent granite pride on the other side of the road.

Remembering those not quite 'Top Secret' police files about the important Professor and his hotel's Irish chef, Ian decided to have a quick look around Professor Osborne's chalet.

Before reaching the blacksmith's he turned left, cycled under the railway bridge then dismounted and pushed his bike up the steep track that led to and past the Territorial Army armoury and drill hall. He decided not to go and see Auld Sandy Robertson the Home Guard corporal who was the caretaker there.

It was fine to meet old army veteran Sandy, but it was damn near impossible to get away from him until he'd finished telling all his old familiar tales of his adventures in the Boer War. Having heard them over and over again, Ian had no desire to listen to Auld Sandy turning the Boer War into the 'Great Bore War' once more, so he turned into the short track that led to Professor Osborne's chalet across from the T.A. armoury.

This large chalet was set in a well-chosen pleasant place. Screened by maturing trees, it stood isolated on the top of a small steep hillock. After checking its locked door and shuttered windows, Ian sat on the inviting wooden seat at the building's West gable.

He gazed around and thought, 'The professor sure knew what he was doing when he built this chalet in such an idyllic spot. The views from this seat bring contented perfection to this perfect place.'

He increased his leisurely pleasure by lighting up one of the few cigarettes he allowed himself each day. A cigar would have been even better, but none were to be had here in rural Perthshire in the midst of this terrible war. (There seemed to be no shortage of large Havanas for dear old Churchill however).

As he gazed around this lush rustic scene with the first blush of Autumnal brightness beginning to subdue the greens, it was sad to think that this beautiful peaceful scene was in effect an aberration, an oasis set in the endless desert of this Second World War's limitless death and destruction.

After giving a solemn sigh, Ian directed his thoughts back to happier and calmer pre-war days. Pre-three wars actually! Pre-Sandy's Boer War, the First World War and this ongoing Second World War.

Down there on the green sward of the Lady's Dell was where he, an innocent late-

Victorian boy, had enjoyed many Sunday-School picnics, and races on always sunny Saturdays, and in the adjoining recreation ground he'd had many boyish thrills on the high flying swings. But never on a Sunday!

His parents had gently explained that these innocent swings were padlocked each Sunday to save children from the heinous sin of enjoying any pleasures on the sacrosanct Sabbath.

Of course that small nine-hole golf course squeezed between these forbidden swings and the River Tummel was also strictly not for use on the Sabbath. It would never do to have irate golfers cursing on this Holy Day as their ill-judged ball landed not on the riverside green but in the river.

There was no salmon fishing at that enticing wee river on the Sabbath either, nor on any other Scottish river. But this time the pleasure-denying injunction was wise, it ensured that on one day per week the returning salmon were unmolested by nets or rods.

Guided by years of fishing experience, Ian's searching gaze followed the fast flowing

Tummel down from his own Glen Hotel's salmon beat to where the next stretch of river belonged to Fonab Estate. And there, above the steep slope from the river, Fonab Castle towered its noble glory above the surrounding trees. In September afternoon's keen sunlight that Victorian tower-house was a glow of sun-warmed red sandstone. Its blushing beauty rivalled the gay display of the autumnal trees.

Ian smiled, 'Oh, I have to admit it, the warm glowing sandstone of that noble pile puts all other Pitlochry buildings, including my own hotel, in the shade. The Sandemans must have spared no expense in buying and railroading in all that glorious red sandstone.

It amused him to think that the Sandeman family had been wealthy enough to buy Fonab Estate and build impressive Fonab Castle thanks to the booming sales of their ports and sherries all through the 19th century.

Their pre-dinner sherry had been genteelly sipped from dainty glasses by oh so prim and proper Victorian ladies. Their after dinner ports were quite a different story. They had been oh so insatiably gulped by 'portly' Victorian gentlemen not by successive glass, but by successive bottle. These port-guzzling gluttonous gentlemen paid the price not only in cash, but in agonising gout.

'Just as well I don't like port,' Ian thought. 'These damn pains in my aching auld knees are bad enough without the hell of gout.'

As he continued gazing around this peaceful scene seemingly so far removed from war and all the horrors of war he was well aware that for him, as for so many other British parents, there was always that unspoken fear buried deep in each anxious mind that one day their worst hidden horror would burst to frantic life and they would receive that dreaded telegram from the War Office, the Admiralty or the Air Ministry informing them 'with deep regret' that their son had been 'Killed in Action'.

He once again sighed, 'Yes, that dreadful dread is rarely spoken of, but in countless silent minds that dread is never dead.'

Then casting his mind back to an earlier anxious year, he smiled, 'Anyway this calm peaceful scene was not so peaceful or calm one night early in August. 1940, that grim time of the threatened German invasion.'

An unseen Luftwaffe plane had dropped four bombs on Fonab Moor some way above Fonab Castle. The savage shattering explosions sent a herd of well antlered stags into a wild stampede of high leaping speed while some nearby sheep became a clumsy riot of urgent panic.

Next morning Old Donnie, the estate's brought out of retirement gamekeeper, inspected the four large bomb-craters on 'his' grouse moor. He gasped, 'Och, what terrible bloody destruction!' He then grinned, 'Och, the rain'll soon turn them into braw pools for the ducks and snipe.'

Searching around where a blizzard of grouse feathers were entangled in thick heather he found two dead red grouse. He examined them. There was no blood, no visible wounds, but both birds had lost most of their feathers.

'By God,' Donnie gasped, 'yon bomb blasts hae fair plucked this braw brace o' grouse.' He then indignantly added, 'Och, but trust thae unsporting Hun bastards tae kill grouse afore the correct "Glorious Twelfth"'

When Ian heard old Donnie telling this tale he'd laughed, 'By God, Donnie, it might be a braw way o' plucking your grouse, but isn't it just a wee bit drastic?'

Then the following year five German bombs had been dropped near Enoch Dhu. The fierce mingled explosions had been alarming, but no real damage was done.

And early this year (1943) a solitary bomb had smashed and snapped trees in Balnacree Wood.

From the 'gen' he'd gathered through friends in the Royal Observer Corps, and his own Home Guard sources, it seemed to Ian that these bombs dropped near Pitlochry had not been aimed at the town.

He knew that German pilots had been ordered to bomb the vital aluminium factories at Fort William and Kinlochleven, but finding these targets – unsurprisingly

– obscured by thick clouds and heavy rain, scattered their bombs more or less at random. Perhaps these weary pilots, operating almost at the limit of their twin-engined Heinkel's range, had been attracted by an illicit gleam of light flowing from some un-properly blacked-out farmhouse window. Or had they seen the impossible to conceal alluring red glow from a steam train on the Perth to Inverness line as the fireman shovelled more coals into the glaring red-hot furnace?

Were these confused German pilots taking in reverse The Road to the Isles as they followed the shimmery gleams of Loch Rannoch and Loch Tummel from Lochaber towards their eager sought airfields in German-occupied Holland?

Sitting thinking of these things, Ian remembered what was by far the most interesting and could have been the most tragic of those Luftwaffe visits to the Pitlochry district.

This time, in early April this year, there had been no violent explosions, no plucked dead grouse, no panicking sheep or deer. There had not even been normal bombs' scary whistling warnings. Unseen, unheard, this latest menace had drifted down with sinister stealth.

Even when the German parachute-mine landed in farmer Jock Cameron's field to the East of Edradour Distillery there was no explosion, no sound except the large silk parachute's rustling, sighing whispers as it deflated. And there that unexploded mine lay on the dewy grass like a huge grey-black slug, its two tons of high explosives an awesome evil menace.

As, early that morning, farmer Jock Cameron walked down with feed for his cows in that field he was surprised not to see the beasts awaiting him at the gate. 'Where hae a' the coos got tae, Ben?' he asked his ear-cocked collie. Then man and also mystified dog were amazed to see the five cows standing in a semi-circle around a strange large object lying on the grass, their inquisitive slobbery noses and wide staring innocent eyes all concentrated on that fantastic thing. When morning's playful breeze coaxed the parachute into sudden fluttery movement the cows backed away in startled fright.

Seeing his wife feeding the hens, Jock shouted, 'Come and see this queer thing, Jeannie.'

'God save us!' she exclaimed. 'Whit's yon awfa muckle thing?'

'Och, it's only a bloody big Jerry bomb lass.' He then laughed, 'Aye, an' yon bonnie parachute silk wid mak a real braw muckle pair o' bloomers fir ye, wouldn't it, lass?'

His buxom, fourteen stone, bright faced wife's ever ready laughter drowned out her husband's mirth as she gasped, 'Och, be quiet you muckle damn fool!'

She then asked, 'Whit are we going tae dae aboot yon devilish thing?'

'Och weel, first o' a' I'll get Ben tae gae real canny an' move the coos awa' frae yon damn bomb an' oot o' the field. Then I'll gae doon tae Edradour Distillery an' get the manager tae phone the polis.'

Once Inspector Grant received that phone call he, after checking that it really was a German parachute-mine, set all necessary procedures into action. The bomb-disposal unit at the Black Watch barracks in Perth were notified. So was Ian, as commander of the local Home Guard.

Soon the police and Home Guard had the area around that dangerous unexploded mine quarantined off, all humans, cows, sheep and horses moved away and – at a discrete distance – a watchful guard was kept on that sinister silent menace.

To those not directly involved in those exciting activities wild rumours made up for the lack of accurate knowledge. Rumours that at first were held to be gospel truths. It was stated as a definite fact that Edradour Distillery had been bombed and was now a smoking ruin.

A group of 'auld worthies' ensconced in 'their' corner near the open fire of the public bar of Pitlochry's Fisher's Hotel were hoping to get "fou and unco happy", although it was damn hard to get really 'fou' in these grim years of watered-down wartime beers and a terrible shortage of whisky, but they'd try their best.

When they heard the devastating 'news'

about the distillery they were distraught at the thought of all that grand Edradour whisky going up in flames.

The oldest and loudest of those boozy old friends well remembered when, early in the war, a large bonded warehouse in Edinburgh had been bombed by these despicable Germans and over a million gallons of pure malt whisky had been destroyed. He passionately shouted, 'Oh thae bloody Huns! I bet you Adolf Bloody Hitler has ordered his damn Luftwaffe pilots tae destroy all oor whisky distilleries! It's just whit a non-smoking, teetotal vegetarian like that bastard would bloody well do, isn't it?'

His sage auld audience nodded their whole-hearted agreement then puffed at their old pipes and sipped more watery beer.

When they later heard the great news that Edradour Distillery was intact and was still in full production their rejoicing was unbounded. They celebrated with even more watered-down beer and drooly dreams of glorious post-war years when there would be real strong beers and an abundance of whisky.

10

When the army's two bomb-disposal experts arrived Inspector John Grant and Major Ian Gray were surprised at how young these brave soldiers were – or appeared to be. The captain seemed little more than a slim, fresh-faced youth. The young sergeant's more solid bulk and strong confident Glasgow accent were more reassuring.

Then John and Ian noted the one ribbon on the young captain's khaki tunic – the ribbon of the M.C. (Military Cross) and they both knew that whatever that officer might lack in years he must more than make up for in experience and bravery.

The sergeant also wore one medal ribbon – the M.M. (Military Medal). Those two medals were awarded for similar acts of bravery, but of course it would never do for non-commissioned other ranks to wear the same medal as officers, and so the British Army continued its class distinction even in its recognition of bravery.

Ian and John led the captain and sergeant to the large unexploded parachute-mine. After examining 'their' mine the young officer grinned, 'Oh, this type of mine is a familiar old friend. It doesn't pose much of a challenge. We shouldn't have any trouble defusing it.'

Pointing at the metal-covered small neat hole near the centre of the mine, the sergeant grinned, 'Aye, that fusing hole is perfect positioned for us to get to it and defuse it. Aye, this time this mine should be a "piece of cake"!'

The captain nodded, 'Yes, I agree.' The two experts exchanged remembering glances. 'Yes, it's a different matter entirely when we have to roll a blasted mine over to get at its fusing hole.'

Very impressed by these young men's confident modest bravery, Ian said, 'It must take real strong nerves to roll those two tons or so of high explosives over'.

The sergeant gave what might have been a slightly nervous laugh, 'Aye, it can be a wee bit hairy! A damn sight tougher than merely "rolling out the barrel" as in yon jolly song.'

'Now, gentlemen,' the captain said, 'you better get out of the way and leave us experts to it.'

'Yes, of course,' Ian agreed, 'we'll go and wait over at that ditch.'

Again the young captain grinned. He pointed, 'No, you better go further away to that more distant hedge.' He then solemnly added, 'Just in case!'

Lying at that hedge Ian and John keenly watched those two bomb-disposal soldiers go about their dangerous work. They were impressed by the calm unhurried way the brave experts went about what must surely be a nerve-wracking task. Even for them, watching from a safe distance, they felt the strain of the terrible fear that just one simple mistake could end in a disastrous explosion.

John spoke in an awed whisper, 'Those brave young men go about their daunting task as calmly as a couple of surgeons performing a very delicate operation, don't they?'

Ian's reply was also whispered, 'Aye, they do.'

After a thoughtful pause he added, 'Oh but there's one huge difference between skilled surgeons and these bomb-disposal experts. If surgeons make a mistake only the poor patient dies. If these young soldiers make a mistake they die!'

Then vivid memories of hideous sights in the last war made him add, 'They become nothing but splattered mincemeat.'

As if awed to silence these two older men said not another word as spellbound they watched these two younger men continue their intricate painstaking work.

After a tense fifteen minutes that seemed much longer to these silent watchers, the young captain's anxious face burst into beaming smiles. He beckoned them over while the sergeant raised his arms and clasped his hands above his head in a boxer's triumphant display.

'There, it's safely defused,' the captain said. He gently patted the ugly large mine, 'It's now as innocent as a new born babe.'

To help those relaxing men further relax, Ian drew a small silver hip-flask from a pocket and handed it to the young officer. 'Here, have a good dram, captain. You both certainly deserve one.'

The captain smiled his thanks and gratefully drank. He handed the flask to his eager waiting Scottish sergeant

The sergeant gulped a generous dram then gave an appreciative sigh as he – perhaps somewhat reluctantly – handed the small flask back to its owner, 'Ah that's a real grand malt, sir, thank you.'

As John took his turn at the flask he laughed, 'Oh, Ian, I hope this isn't black market whisky you're handing round.'

'No, it's certainly not!' He too laughed, 'If it was black-market whisky I would hardly be giving it to you – a police inspector – would I?'

He explained to the amused young soldiers, 'My wife and I own a Pitlochry hotel. Now and then we manage to get some scarce whisky. We keep it for special occasions.'

He raised his returned flask and toasted these brave young men. 'And thanks to both you experts this truly is a special occasion. I thank you not only on behalf of John and myself but of all the farmers living nearby whose lives and houses had been threatened by that parachute-mine.'

The sergeant modestly grinned, 'Och, it's all in the day's work for us.'

The captain then said, 'I'll need to phone and arrange for our special crane and truck to come and take this mine away.'

'Why don't you come with me to my hotel and phone from there?' Ian suggested. He glanced at his watch, 'I'll give you both a bit of late lunch too.'

'Yes, that would be grand. Thank you. Oh, but we don't have any ration coupons for our food.'

'Oh that's no problem. I'll give you food

that's not rationed. How do you fancy a piece of fresh River Tummel salmon?'

'Oh that would be wonderful.'

With lips that were almost drooling the sergeant agreed, 'Aye, fresh salmon will be a real treat.'

Sitting on this well positioned seat at the end of Professor Osborne's chalet with its views over the River Tummel, Ian remembered the eager appetites those two young, healthy, bomb-disposal soldiers had displayed as they ate their generous helpings of grilled salmon. As he had watched them appreciatively eat he could almost see the last of their nervous tensions ease away now that they had again proved that they could safely defuse these German parachute-mines.

'Yes,' he thought, 'that happened about six months ago and there's been no further Luftwaffe activity over the Pitlochry district since then, and as far as I know, there's been little, or no, further German bombing of any other parts of Scotland either, so surely there's a good chance that those two brave young men are still alive.'

He glanced at his watch, 'Oh this leisurely sitting and quiet reminiscing is very pleasant, but I suppose I'd better get back to the hotel and to work.'

As he neared the railway bridge he heard the rumbling thunder of an approaching train. He stopped cycling and dismounted. Standing staring he waited to see what wartime train would appear. A crowded troop-train? An ammunition laden goods train? An even more crowded passenger train with its determined civilians replying "Yes!" to those almost accusing official posters at every British railway station which – trying to save coal – asked, 'Is your journey really necessary?'

The approaching train's thunder grew even louder. He saw plumes of grey/black smoke and mists of hissing steam. Although large and powerful the L.M.S (London Midland and Scottish) locomotive appeared to be labouring as it hauled its heavy burden of flat truck after flat truck, each laden with fresh felled, neat stacked large logs.

As in the last war, Scotland's forests were being denuded to meet the needs of modern war's insatiable greed.

Ian waved and the white haired train driver gave a cheery toot.

Ian wondered if that skilled old driver, and even perhaps his demoted locomotive, were feeling the ignominy of this mundane goods train's work?

Was he nostalgically remembering pre-war years when this mighty steam machine and he had sped with excitement and bright pride, a thundering express on the London to Glasgow line?

Was his memory winging him further back to his younger years when he played a minor role in the great Romance of Steam?

In other older L.M.S. engines he'd helped speed the non-stop overnight sleeper trains from crowded Euston Station to the sporty charms of the Scottish Highlands. In early August those first-class sleeper carriages had been for the exclusive use of wealthy sporting gentry, their guns, dogs and rods. With what eager anticipation those trigger-happy landed gentry hurried North to be on their grouse moors in time for the Glorious Twelfth.

When that old train driver gasped dreamy reminiscent sighs it seemed to him that his faithful old locomotive joined in with its own weary steamy sighs. But surely by this stage of this endless seeming Second World War both ageing driver and labouring machine were resigned to doing their mundane goods-train tasks? Were they quietly proud to be doing this necessary ceaseless work? Doing their bit for Britain's war effort; doing their duty to King and Country.

As sooty smoke, hissing steam and rumbling noise faded away Ian resumed his cycling.

Pitlochry's part of the A9 road seemed to be in a pleasant lazy after lunch mood. There were even fewer than the usual few trucks and horse drawn carts on the move. There were no more army convoys. The only military traffic that passed Ian was one dark blue Royal Navy truck that sped through the sleepy wee Perthshire town as if in urgent hurry to get to the distant sea. The few, ever hopeful housewives seemed almost half-hearted as they went from shop to shop in search for some treat: some fresh arrived un-rationed food.

As he cycled past the familiar row of neat old grey houses he approvingly noted the wisdom of an old ginger cat as it curled in cosy bliss on the top of the sun-warned low grey wall enclosing one of the tiny front gardens. That wise feline acknowledged his almost silent passing by only half opening its enquiring eyes.

Ian again enjoyed the usual pleasure of free-wheeling down the gentle slope of the side road that led direct to his Glen Hotel. Then, as he returned his cycle to the hotel's garage where his immobile old Rover car took up most of the space, he reminded himself of the need to be extra wary when he next met his Irish chef, Daniel Bailey. He knew it might be quite a strain to make sure there appeared to be no change in his attitude to that Irishman who might be quite innocent, might be absolutely no threat to that top scientist, Professor Osborne. Or might – as Special Branch seemed to fear – that Irishman be a real threat to the professor?

This unique situation might be made clearer if only Ian knew what secret scientific work Professor Osborne was engaged on. Was it really of vital importance to Britain's war effort? Was his top-secret work really important enough that the Germans might send a secret Irish agent to try to kill him? Surely that seemed unlikely? Surely that had a touch of a far-out John Buchan spy thriller?

Ian was well aware that, apart from keeping these hidden suspicions from Daniel Bailey, he must also keep them from his wife. This might be a much more difficult task. He all too well knew how mysteriously powerful, were Anne's intuitive gifts. When she first met Daniel she'd felt an instinctive quiver of slight unease, of something not quite right about him.

That feeling had not been strong enough for Anne to object to Ian's decision to hire him as chef. But if Anne ever discovered these Special Branch rational masculine suspicions about Daniel Bailey to add to her own strange intuitive feminine unease about him, things would be very different. She might demand that Ian sack him.

Later that afternoon Ian, Anne and Daniel met to decide the ration-restricted menu for tonight's dinner for the hotel guests. Ian was pleased at how well he'd passed this first test of concealing any hints of suspicions about the Irish chef. Before leaving the hotel's gleaming roomy kitchen Ian said, 'Oh, by the way, Daniel, I haven't forgotten the day's salmon fishing on the River Tummel I promised you. I'll make sure you get it before the fishing season ends. As I expect you already know, we have two special guests, a Naval Officer and an Air Force Officer and their wives staying with us all this week. Those two officers are very keen salmon fishers. They hope their fishing will help them relax from the trials and strains of their stressful wartime duties. So they will get the best of the hotel's fishing all the time they're here. I think that's only fair, don't you?'

'Aye, of course', Daniel said in his pleasant gentle Irish brogue. He grinned, 'Nothing but the best for those brave... those brave "officers and gentlemen"!'

When Ian left the kitchen he uneasily thought of that hesitation in Daniel's reply. Had he been about to say, "those brave English officers and gentlemen"? Did this hint at a concealed dislike of these English officers?

Ian knew that a real dislike, or even an actual hatred, of the English was fairly widespread in the Irish Republic. Was that how Daniel secretly felt? And did he have a deep concealed dislike of us Scots too? Despite him having two brothers serving in the British army could be really be a pro-German agent?

Ian wondered if he was becoming paranoid because of that confidential Special Branch file on Daniel. It was all too easy to get into an unjustified over-suspicious state.

But what if a deceptive Daniel really was a menace to Professor Osborne?

Thank God that at present the Professor is not here. But when he does arrive for a holiday at his Pitlochry chalet the threat of Daniel's possible deception might become clearer. Perhaps our unobtrusive Home Guard and police protection of the professor might better be strengthened.

11

Ian again met Commander Richardson and Group Captain Williams as they returned to his hotel after another successful day's salmon fishing at the hotel's pools on the River Tummel. He again congratulated them on their success: one salmon of almost eleven pounds and another of nine pounds for the Commander. Only one for the Group Captain, but what he lacked in numbers he more than made up for by his solitary fish weighing thirty two pounds.

So, success depending on weight, this time the R.A.F. beat the Royal Navy in those officers daily fishing bet. The Commander would have to buy the pre-dinner drinks this evening. As he joined in the two officers animated talk as they re-lived their day of successful fishing, Ian was pleased to see how their all-engrossing fly-fishing had again worked its relaxing magic, had eased some of the tensions from their smiling faces. Commander Richardson especially seemed now much more at ease.

Ian remembered the shock he'd got at the appearance of the Commander when he'd arrived at the hotel after almost a year's absence. His hair – bypassing grey – had gone direct from brown to bright white. Tight strain lines clustered around his sunken eyes and etched their way to his grim mouth. He had lost weight and added twenty years to his age.

The Commander gave no explanation for these drastic changes. But his wife, in cosy, intimate, confidential chats with Ian's wife, Anne, revealed something of the almost ceaseless naval ordeals that had so aged her middle-age husband.

Over pleasant cups of afternoon tea or morning cups of not so pleasant wartime 'coffee' made mainly from dandelion weeds, she told of her nervous apprehension each time the Commander went on yet another dangerous voyage.

In command of his grand new Royal Navy destroyer he'd helped protect three successive Russian convoys. And no convoys were more important and more dangerous than these Arctic ones that took urgent needed British and American war supplies to our desperately fighting Soviet Allies. As each of these convoys forced its way around the North of German-occupied Norway to reach Murmansk they came under fierce attacks from German U-boats and aircraft. As if these deadly attacks were not had enough there was always the terrible threat from the formidable German battleship the *Tirpitz* as it lurked in its northerly Norwegian lair ready to pounce on any passing convoy.

But often these terrible human menaces were overshadowed by the ever present menace of the arctic weather. Severe winter storms would thump mountainous waves of monstrous weight over shuddering ships. Freezing spray would coat moaning superstructures with tenacious clinging layers of thick ice that had to be labouriously chipped away before ships got precariously top-heavy. Blinding blizzards would scream in direct from the North Pole and, seeming with evil glee, slash at duffel-hooded sailors exhausted faces.

At action stations much of the time, with no real deep sleep, little proper food, only the monotonous 'KYE' diet of cocoa and corned-beef sandwiches, and always the numbing chill of the freezing Arctic, plus the constant threat of death, these Russian winter convoys were a real White Hell.

For Commander Richardson there was the extra strain of the heavy responsibility of commanding a Royal Navy warship in the midst of a savage war. This was what he, a professional officer in the regular navy, had been trained for. This he did in the Royal Navy's ingrained tradition of 'The Nelson Spirit' that faced the most daunting dangers with resolute leadership and bravery.

One of these convoys was trial enough for most sailors, so after surviving three successive winter Arctic convoys it was surely little wonder that the commander's hair had suddenly gone pure white.

Group Captain Williams face showed less signs of stress. There were a few fresh etched lines around his eyes, but he had lost no weight and his neat black hair had not yet gone white, it merely displayed some not-unattractive flecks of silver. He was one of the R.A.F. Bomber Command pilots who, having completed a thirty mission tour of bombing duty over German targets had volunteered to do another full bombing tour. He had done this after a well-deserved 'rest' when he'd helped train fresh young novice pilots. Perhaps the fact of him seeing almost as many deaths from training crashes as he'd seen from German flak and night-fighters was a definite factor in his decision. But surely he must have known that the chance of him surviving yet another thirty bombing missions against the ever increasing, even more deadly German homeland defences must be quite small. But he did! He'd survived unharmed even although many times his bombing target was the most distant, most heavily defended of all German cities – Berlin.

After being made Commanding Officer of one of the many large R.A.F. Bomber Command airfields set in the drab flat countryside around Lincoln he'd been more or less grounded by more senior officers. Despite the official disapproval he still occasionally flew one more bombing mission. Perhaps this was one way he could assuage his conscience as, night after night, he sent young aircrews in their large, bomb-laden Lancasters to attack heavily defended targets in Germany knowing that one, two, or sometimes even more, would not come back. This searing knowledge that he was sending some of these brave young men (many merely 19 years old) to their deaths often felt a much greater strain on him than taking part in these bombing raids himself.

He, their Commanding Officer, must never show himself getting too distressed by these ceaseless deaths. Yet if he seemed too phlegmatic, never appeared to be in the least upset by these tragic deaths he could be disapprovingly thought of as being a real callous old bastard.

None who thought of him with silent disapproval had the least suspicion of how he felt each time he, alone in his commanding officer's office, wrote all those letters of condolence to stricken parents of killed pilots and aircrew. Then he flew one more voluntary bombing mission that finally decided him that he'd do no more. On this last trip he'd, in R.A.F. jargon, 'almost bought it' – 'had almost gone for a Burton': almost been killed. When nearing the Dutch coast after another familiar 'milk-run' to the often bombed Ruhr, that heart of heavy German industry, his Lancaster had been shot up by a Luftwaffe night-fighter. Two engines were knocked out but he thought he'd make it back to England on the remaining two.

Thanks to his piloting skills they came in almost on a direct line for a welcoming airfield's well-lit runway. He made an almost perfect landing, made it only just in time for as their wheels touched down their coughing third engine spluttered a final weary sigh and died.

For Group Captain Williams from then on there was no longer the stress of night-time flying on hazardous bombing missions. Now he only faced the harrowing task of sending ever more brave young airmen to early deaths.

The two officers returned to their hotel bedrooms to change out of their de rigueur fishing tweeds then have a pre-dinner bath, possibly most patriotically in only the recommended wartime austerity depth of no more than five inches of not too wastefully hot water.

Ian went to his office to attend to some of the ever increasing flood of new Government rules and regulations. He thought this endless increase in official bumph was more likely to stifle the war effort with red tape rather than help it.

Before getting down to those official forms he suddenly thought of another officer. An Army Lieutenant who with his new wife had been guests last week. What a contrast that young lieutenant was from this week's two older officers with their vast experience of this war's awful horrors, its desperate dangers, its cruel stresses and strains. Its deaths.

Like so many in the British Army that young officer had not yet been in any military action. He had yet to face the ordeal of his first baptism of enemy fire.

This lack of any fighting experience was even truer of the bulk of the American Army now stationed in Britain. Many of these young, untested American soldiers had not even seen the sea until military conscription took them from the prairies of their inland states to cross the North Atlantic on one of these huge troop-ships, the *Queen Mary* and the *Queen Elizabeth*.

For almost two years many of these untested young British and American soldiers had been practising amphibious landing at various British beaches.

Ian remembered that young Army Lieutenant telling how realistic was this constant training. Much live ammunition was fired at them. The officer had grinned, 'Not actually fired at us! The artillery shells exploded harmlessly in the wide sea. The machine-gun bullets sped above our wading bodies and apprehensive heads.'

He paused them quietly said, 'Oh, but it will be another matter entirely when we wade ashore on some heavily defended French beach. German guns will accurately aim at our landing craft, then veteran Hun machine-gunners will try to send bullets thudding into our vulnerable bodies.'

Neither that young officer or Ian knew it, but this was a constant worry for Prime Minister Churchill, British General

Montgomery and American General Eisenhower as they anxiously observed some of these practice amphibious landings.

How would those untested young British and American soldiers react when they were eventually put to the grim test?

Churchill especially was burdened with a terrible weight of dread. Ghosts from the last war still haunted him. Then in August last year there was that other amphibious disaster. The trial landing at German-defended Dieppe. The four thousand Canadian soldiers killed, wounded or captured.

Yet Churchill well knew that these past disasters would be as nothing compared to the scale of disaster if the huge joint British and American landings planned for next year should also fail. He was also all too well aware that if – as he prayed they would – next year's landings were successful the casualties on the first day alone were expected to be somewhere between 10,000 and 20,000 British, Americans, Canadian and other allied soldiers, sailors and airmen.

Of course the likelihood of that dreadful number of casualties was kept a strict dark secret from all those about to take part in these landings.

Ian felt deep empathy for that anxious young Army Lieutenant who could very easily become one of those tragic casualties. He understood his hidden secret fears. All too clearly he remembered his own nervous hidden fears in the last war (that war that was going to end all wars!) just over twenty years ago.

He had been a young, untested subaltern in the Black Watch: that regiment which – according to their Regimental Sergeant Major – was one of the oldest and also the best regiment, with the bravest soldiers, in the entire British Army.

After some weary months in Flanders digging practice trenches their regiment was sent up to the front line. For Ian, that as yet untested young officer, there had been a hidden fear that he might not be up to the terrible test of leading his men 'over the top' and guiding them across 'no man's land' to the Hun trenches. He had imagination enough to guess at how eagerly Death must be waiting out there. Yes, bloodthirsty Death must be waiting with Bated Breath! They were given generous gulps of extra strong rum. Their massed guns ceased their nerve-shredding thunderous roar. There was a short apprehensive wait.

Then young Lieutenant Ian Gray led his men 'over the top' and across 'no man's land'.

Hun machine guns swept their hail of death at those Black Watch soldiers advancing precariously slowly as they floundered through the vile Flanders mud. The British attack soon petered out as all too many brave young men savagely died. After seeing their Sergeant-Major and then his friend, Lieutenant Fergusson, being shot down by these machine-guns that swept their relentless death from behind almost intact Hun barbed-wire, Ian wisely decided it would not be supreme bravery, but utter madness to continue struggling forward to almost certain pointless death.

Shouting orders for his nearest soldiers to follow him, he jumped, slipped and slid into the safety of a large, deep and muddy shell crater. He and the corporal and the three privates who slid in with him grinned with relief at being out of sight of those hellish Hun machine-guns. As they sorted themselves out in this safe haven the burly older corporal made tension-relieving crude jokes about the obscene discomforts they all suffered from their kilts and nether regions being soggily plastered with soft cold mud. All the younger soldiers, including Ian, let their appreciative nervous laughter cover their deep distress at the thought of so many of their poor brave comrades lying dead or dying in floods of blood.

Under the blessed cover of night's darkness Ian's group of five survivors made their way back to the British front line. Although appalled by his Battalion's horrendous loss's Ian had the secret satisfaction of knowing that he'd successfully passed the desperate test of his soldiery bravery. He had kept his nerve, had kept his fears well hidden, had set a strong brave example to his surviving men whom, he hoped, would now view him with fresh respect.

Returning from his vivid memories of the last war to the sad realities of this Second World War, Ian wished that young Army Lieutenant equal success when he faced his grim test in next year's amphibious landings in France. He hoped he would survive the war and that his lovely young wife would not become a grief-aged war widow.

He sighed then turned his mind to reading the small print of these latest confusing Government forms.

12

One week later, getting to the end of September, the Glen Hotel like many other Highland hotels was winding down, was getting ready for its wartime winter semi-hibernation.

There were only two guests, retired old Doctor MacPherson and his even older, even frailer wife. Having come here year after year since long before the war, they were treated as grand old friends. They were bright and cheery despite the hidden fears old Mrs. MacPherson confided to Ian's sympathetic wife, Anne.

Their son was also a doctor; they had worried about him while he was serving in the R.A.M.C. (Royal Army Medical Corps) during the First World War when the British Army's medical services in Flanders were often almost overwhelmed by the horrendous flood of casualties. Sometimes their son's forward medical facilities had been within range of Hun artillery and had even been affected by drifting clouds of poison gas.

Their son had survived unscathed, but now his son, their only grandson, was serving as a Medical Officer in the R.A.M.C in this Second World War. So far he was quite safe 'somewhere in England' he, like the bulk of the British Army, was endlessly training for next year's amphibious landings in France.

But his training was something special. His medical team would be one of the first to land soon after the main allied landings so he was being taught emergency surgical skills to attempt to save severely wounded soldiers' lives. He became expert at quick amputations and at urgently patching up the terrible damage bullets and jagged shrapnel did to fragile human flesh.

He was thankful he had a wonderful new ally to help his patched-up patients survive: Doctor Fleming's new wonder drug, Penicillin.

If his father had had this almost miraculous new drug in his war's filthy horrors of mud, dirt, shit and blood, many thousands of wounded British soldiers might well have survived.

He knew this Penicillin was being urgently produced and being stockpiled beside those many empty military hospital beds all waiting for this war's coming flood of wounded British soldiers.

Anne tried to reassure the worried old grandmother, 'Oh, I'm sure he will come through this war just as his father did in his terrible war.' But she secretly, almost despairingly, thought, 'Oh but will he? Oh, when the Hell is this madness of war after war ever going to end?'

With his hotel now almost empty and with no English Officers to disapprove, Ian could now keep his promise to his chef, Daniel Bailey. He would get a day's fishing on the River Tummel.

But, as Ian explained, 'Not on my hotel's beat on the river. A friend who's the Factor on a nearby sporting estate has offered me a day's free fishing for two rods on his estate's part of the Tummel above and below the Tummel Falls. So I will come with you tomorrow and we'll share this grand fishing offer. You agree, Daniel? Or would you prefer to fish by yourself?'

'Oh no, of course not,' Daniel laughed and put on a broader Irish accent, 'Sure but it'll be a real honour to fish with such a dandy fisherman as you, sur!'

Surprised by the Irishman's unusual display of self-mocking humour, Ian echoed his laughter and said, 'Och, Daniel, I don't deserve such grand flattery.'

While Ian had always found Daniel quite friendly (he didn't like to be called 'Dan' and really hated being patronisingly referred to as 'Danny Boy') he was also – most unusual in an Irishman – very reserved and untalkative.

This was especially true whenever some aspect of the ongoing war was mentioned. Some of the hotel staff disliked Daniel's silence when they were warmly greeting news of some fresh Allied victory.

Ian had decided that Daniel was merely displaying his own and his Irish Republic country's neutral stance in this war.

Surely him having two brothers (one of whom had been awarded the Military Medal) serving in the British Army was proof enough of his family's pro-British leanings?

But then there were those dark suspicions in that damn Special Branch secret file that were now ingrained deep in Ian's mind.

Could Daniel really be hiding his true feelings about this war? Could he be a German-supporting agent? Be more or less a Nazi spy?

Oh surely such thoughts were crazy? Surely he was letting his imagination get wildly out of hand? Anyway even if Daniel did pose a real threat to Professor Osborne there was nothing he could do about it at present as the professor was not staying in his Pitlochry chalet.

Actually the professor had never been here during the few months that Daniel had been working at the Glen Hotel. Twice that summer Police Inspector John Grant had notified Ian that the professor was arriving on a few days holiday at his chalet and Ian should arrange unobtrusive Home Guard protection for him. Then on both occasions the professor's holiday was cancelled just before it was about to begin. It seemed that the top secret scientific work Professor Osborne was engaged in was so vitally important that he could not be allowed even a few days away from it.

Once again Ian wondered if he would ever learn the professor's secrets and would he ever discover if Daniel Bailey really was a dangerous threat to the professor. Could that pleasant Irish chef hide murderous thoughts deep in his mind? Yet any secret agent would hardly be a good agent if they could not convincingly conceal their true feelings, true intentions.

Ian remembered the only time he'd heard Daniel express his thoughts with eager animation and verbal passion and that was when the two of them had been re-telling favourite old tales about Irish and Scottish salmon and trout fishing.

'Oh, damn it all, I'll try to wholeheartedly enjoy the fishing with Daniel tomorrow but I'll also try to keep alert to any hints that he might not be as he seems.' Ian smiled, 'I'll try to prove myself a better secret agent than Daniel, in the unlikely event that he really is one,'

As Ian and Daniel set out on their day of salmon fishing they seemed as carefree as a couple of eager schoolboys happy to be free of the tyranny of school.

For Ian it was strange not to be taking the usual route on the path from his Glen Hotel past fields of gentle grazing drowsy sheep and innocently inquisitive wide-eyed cattle to the familiar pools on his hotel's beat on the grand wee River Tummel. Instead today Daniel and he were keenly striding out to the entrancing lure of more distant salmon pools, the ones they'd been invited to at the impressive Falls of Tummel. After the recent rains these Falls should be at their enticing best with today's smiling sunshine lighting them with sparkling spray-bright life.

After hurrying down a narrow road's gentle slope they arrived at the old, twin-spanned, grey-stoned Clunie Bridge. Although in eager hurry to get to their salmon pools, these true fishermen had to pause, lean on the old bridge's invitingly wide stone parapet and gaze upstream at the pleasant, fast-flowing River Tummel.

As one they gasped and pointed as two large salmon leapt, arched and splashed their wondrous silvery beauty. 'Come on,' Ian laughed, 'let's get going. More silver beauties will be waiting for us at the Falls Pool'.

So they hurried across the old Clunie Bridge then followed the much, much older Foss Road that snaked along by the west bank of the River Tummel towards the Falls then continued on by Loch Tummel's bonnie south shore. As they came to the old 'Priest's Stone' that stood alone beside the ancient Pictish Foss Road and the fast-flowing river, Ian wondered how Daniel, that Irish Catholic, would react to that stone's carved Christian Cross.

But Daniel merely gave it a cursory glance as he strode past, then he smiled at Ian, 'You can see that I'm a lapsed Catholic, can't you?'

Ian gave a return smile, 'Aye. I noticed that. I suppose I am a lapsed Christian too – a lapsed Protestant.' After a slight pause he continued, 'After all the awful horrors I saw in the last war and the even worse horrors of this ongoing war I find it hard to believe that there's a kind, benevolent, caring God.'

Daniel nodded as if in agreement but said no more.

Soon the old Foss Road climbed above the river and the two men looked down at the Falls of Tummel. Although not very high nor huge these Falls, neatly divided in two by a central jut of solid rock, were truly impressive as they roared, splashed and sprayed their powerful flood of savage glory.

Ian now explained, 'We're only permitted to fish the north side of the river. So we're going across by the Coronation footbridge. It's just a wee bit further on.'

Their journey so far had been mainly under birch, oak and beech trees whose varied summer greens were now reluctantly giving way to autumn's mists, frosts and golden glowing glories. But once across that footbridge they were in a different wooded world: a paradise of evergreen Scots Pines. Some of these tenacious auld trees might even be remnants of Scotland's Ancient Caledonian Forest that once clad most of the Highlands.

As Ian halted and pointed Daniel gasped with delight at his first sight of red squirrels. He open-mouthed gazed at two of those lovely lively wee creatures as they actively scampered and excitedly chattered while they gathered hazel nuts.

Ian had almost to pull him away, 'Come on, Daniel, I know those cute wee squirrels are grand, but those waiting salmon are even grander.'

Soon they were at the first deep, rocky, smooth flowing salmon pool and Ian said, 'There, Daniel, you fish here. I'll go on to the next pool.'

Normal time ceased to exist for Ian as he sent the first cast of his Green Highlander fly on a salmon-enticing curving sweep through the pool's attractive waters. He was engulfed in fishing's ever hopeful timeless glory, was in direct touch with his hunting, fishing ancestors. After an unproductive fishing hour or so he was leaving this pool when he met Daniel proudly proclaiming his success by holding his eight pound salmon aloft in his triumphant hand. They fished from pool to pool without further success then Ian guided Daniel along the narrow rock ledge that took them down towards the roaring Falls of Tummel. This rather precarious route was made reasonably safe thanks to the iron hand-rail bolted to the small sheer cliff. As they stood admiring the thundering wonder of the Falls, a large salmon leapt in an urgent attempt to get up that waterfall and then continue further on. They gave simultaneous sympathetic gasps as the disdainful flood swept the defeated salmon roughly tumbling back down to the deep pool below.

'Do any salmon get up these falls?' Daniel asked.

'No, not many – if any. They don't have to.' Ian pointed, 'There's a much easier route for them over there.'

He led Daniel to the narrow fish-pass (also known as a salmon ladder) that had been blasted and laboriously pick-axed through the heart of solid rock to give salmon easy passage to Lochs Tummel and Rannoch and then to their spawning redds in the desolate peaty wastes of Rannoch Moor.

Daniel was impressed, 'They must have used a lot of gunpowder to blast through that lot.'

'Aye, they did. That was away back in 1910. Those were the loudest explosions many of us locals had ever heard.' Ian paused and gave what might have been a grin, or have been a grimace. 'Oh but just a few years later, from 1914, many of us heard much louder and deadlier explosions. For all too many men of my generation those were the last sounds they ever heard.'

Ian wondered how Daniel would react to this talk going from peace to war, so he waited and keenly watched for his reply. Perhaps it would be revealing.

But Daniel was not very forthcoming. He merely solemnly said, 'Oh yes, all those deaths were terrible.' Then, as if eager to change the subject, he suggested, 'Oh, but shouldn't we be getting on with our salmon fishing?'

'Aye, of course,' Ian replied. Then he thought, 'Aye, but before we do I'll try you with a real test. Something that might make you reveal some of your deepest, most hidden true thoughts, might make it clearer if you might really be a threat to Professor Osborne, or be completely innocent of any pro-German, anti-British sentiments'.

Ian knew the many Irish Catholics, to a greater or lesser degree, hated what they always talked of as the English Establishment and the English Royal Family with its guaranteed Protestant ascendancy, so he led Daniel from that salmon ladder to a nearby solid stone cairn and stood silently beside it.

The Irishman swallowed Ian's un-subtle lure. 'Is this cairn in memory of someone?' he asked.

'Yes, it is. It's a memorial, one of many in her beloved Scottish Highlands, to good old Queen Victoria. Under the tuition of her favourite artist, Landseer, she sat here and painted her dainty watercolours of those impressive Falls of Tummel.'

'Oh, did she,' Daniel quietly said. Then Ian was surprised to see his face flush with what seemed sudden anger. Now no longer quietly, but with fierce furnace heat the Irishman declared, 'Oh, of course it was all right for that fat auld English Bitch and her strait-laced, tight-arsed Bastard Albert to paint pretty pictures of her Beloved Scottish Highlands while catching her salmon and stalking her deer, but turning a blind eye to all the distress, starvation and death that the tragic black years of the Irish Potato Blight was inflicting on her not beloved, but her ignored, benighted Ireland.'

Ian, now more amazed than merely surprised at Daniel's heated outburst, was about to say, 'Oh, I agree. That Irish Potato Blight was a terrible disaster. But, you know, Scotland's West Highlands and Islands were badly affected by that Blight too.'

But as he started to speak he was silenced by Daniels increasingly heated outpourings about his country's historic grievance. 'Aye, that bastard Victoria's shameful neglect of her Ireland's terrible distress made her as guilty as that other bloody English Queen – Virgin Elizabeth who urged her rampaging army to unsparingly plunder, loot and murder all Irish Catholics who resisted her right to rule over Ireland.'

Daniel paused and Ian was again about to speak, but before he could the Irishman, having drawn a refreshing breath, got passionately going on probably Ireland's most hated Englishman: Oliver Cromwell. 'Then that bloody evil Devil, Cromwell, with his blood-thirsty Puritanical Protestant army was not satisfied with merely carrying out widespread murderous slaughter, but also vented their religious hate on poor old Ireland's noble Abbeys, Cathedrals and chapels.'

Gasping for breath and seeming trying to get his emotions under control, Daniel fell silent.

So this time Ian might be allowed to speak. But before he did he inwardly smiled at the thought that if such passionate outpourings come from a 'Lapsed Irish Catholic,' as Daniel had described himself to be, how much more passionate would such outbursts be when coming from a true Irish Catholic Believer!

However he kept that thought to himself and said, 'Oh, Daniel, I know all about Cromwell too. Scotland's Abbeys, Cathedrals and even many humble wee kirks suffered from his desecrations and plunderings as well, you know. He even tried to steal Scotland's ancient Royal Crown jewels too.'

Observing Daniel's now calmer, perhaps rather shamefaced expression, Ian thought he'd try to further ease his lessening tension with some humour, so he smiled, 'Yes, Daniel, that auld devil Cromwell ruined many Scottish things too. There's even an old music hall song about his ruinous doings. Auld thespian hags used to shrilly sing their jocular plaintive woes of being, 'One of the Ruins that Cromwell knocked about a bit!'

Daniel gave an appreciative smile, 'Aye, Ian, I've heard that ripe old music hall song too. I'm sorry if I got just a wee bit carried away there with all my anti-English rantings.'

Then with what seemed genuine sincerity he said, 'I assure you that I feel quite different about you Scottish people. We Irish and you Scots have a lot in common. Don't we have a rather similar history of centuries of struggling against English tyranny?'

He paused, then with eyes proudly gleaming with achieved victory, rather tauntingly asked, 'Now that Ireland – or most of Ireland – has gained its long-sought freedom from English rule, why doesn't Scotland do the same?'

That's a good question, Ian silently acknowledged, one he'd sometimes pondered. Heart and brain were divided. Emotional heart was all for Scottish Freedom. Unsentimental brain was all for commercial gain. The majority of his hotel's guests were well-off English, including many retired blimpish Colonels and dyed-in-the-wool old Royal Navy officers. Any suggestion of us Scots breaking away from the United Kingdom would be a real red rag to a bull for them. They might even give up their beloved salmon fishing on Scottish rivers.

So he merely said, 'Oh, Daniel we've this terrible war to fight first. To fight and win. We'll see what happens to Scotland in the post-war years.'

'Aye, sure you've this war to fight. But can you be so sure who's going to win?'

Taken aback by that unexpected question Ian gasped, 'Oh surely there can't be any doubt about that. The grand British, American, and Russia allies will win it. They must!' He wondered if Daniel had unintentionally betrayed some pro-German leaning in that seeming doubting of the certainty of an Allied victory.

For a few silent elongated moments he stared at Daniel then said, 'Oh, Daniel, surely your two brothers who're fighting in the British Army will have no doubts about who's going to win this war.'

It was Daniel's turn to be taken aback. He gasped, 'How do you know about my brothers? I've never mentioned them to you.'

'Oh bugger it,' Ian thought, 'I've put my foot in it! I read about his brothers in that Special Branch secret file; that file he knows nothing about. Oh God, how easy it is to make mistakes in this strange damn game of secrets and deceptions.'

Then he thought of a way out of what seemed a real faux pas. He smiled, 'No, Daniel, you've never mentioned your brothers directly to me, but you must have spoken about them to some of the hotel's staff, then they mentioned them to my wife. She in turn talked about them to me.'

'Oh, I see.' Daniel seemed quite satisfied with this answer.

Surely he could have no suspicions of Ian having read about his brothers in that secret file? Or could he! Could Daniel really be a definite threat to Professor Osborne, or was he truly as innocent as he seemed? But why had he asked, 'can you be sure who's going to win this war?"

Ian's rather confused mind suddenly flashed back to his experiences in the trenches during the last war. That war had been quite straightforward for British infantry soldiers in Flanders. You tried to kill the Huns. The Huns try to kill you. There was no ambiguity there!

This present conflict's terrible doubts over Daniel's innocence or guilt, all this possible 'cloak and dagger' stuff was a different type of war entirely. Was it possible that Daniel had hidden suspicions about Ian's suspicions about him?

Suppressing a weary sigh, Ian thought, 'Oh bugger all these damn uncertainties, I'll get on with the salmon fishing. At least

I know that Daniel is sincere in his passion for fishing.'

So while Daniel fished the large, deep, fast flowing, white foaming pool below the Falls of Tummel, Ian went to a smaller, neater, calmer pool a little further downstream.

As he started fishing Ian had high hopes that this was where he'd belatedly catch his first salmon of the day. Yet even while concentrating on trying to catch these elusive fish he also, more or less subconsciously, drank in the beauty of the surrounding autumnal scene.

The hurrying Tummel drew his gaze to where the River Garry, now free of the narrow confines of the Pass of Killiecrankie, rushed its flood into its larger rival.

While larch, birch, beech and oak, cloaked these twin Perthshire rivers with the brilliant glow of Autumn's golden show, all these glorious trees were quite upstaged by the vivid flamboyant display put on by one large old Rowan.

Standing in isolated splendour near the foot of Ian's pool that shameless old harlot flouted her seductive charms. The lipstick reds of her vivid leaves tried to outdo the bawdy crimson rouge of her countless berries. As if in mock modesty, bunches of these berries coyly drooped under the sinful weight of their irresistible allure.

Little wonder that, half driven mad with feeding lust, Blackbirds and Thrushes were hopelessly besotted. Little wonder that, gluttonously greedy, they would try to gobble the lot before large flocks of Fieldfares and Redwings flew in from Norway.

Watching these insatiable birds, Ian thought of the imminent arrival of their Scandinavian rivals. How wise of these Fieldfares and Redwings to wing their way to Scotland, all innocently unaware that they flew over extensive German and British North Sea minefields. He contrasted their innocent flight with the most un-innocent flight of some humans from Norway: the fanatic Nazi Luftwaffe pilots who had brought nothing but destruction and blood- red death to Scotland.

Ian sighed, no matter how one tried, it was quite impossible to get this ongoing war completely out of your daytime mind. And all too often this war invaded your night-time mind with nightmare horrors even worse than daylight's awful realities.

Yes, no matter how gloriously one was surrounded with nature's beauty you were still aware that even this remote idyllic countryside was still part of the same mad world that was tearing itself apart in this, the worst, the most bloodthirsty war of any.

Then Ian's eye and mind were brought back to that seductive auld Rowan.

A greedy feeding blackbird, its distended crop threatening to burst its bulging breast, knocked some berries from an overhanging branch into the pool below.

An intrigued Ian saw a large salmon gently rise and suck down one of these floating berries. Was that vivid red berry irresistible to salmon too? It seemed so, for as he keenly watched, that salmon again rose, again sucked down a second berry.

Knowing that salmon do not normally feed in fresh water, he felt quite sure that this unique fish would quickly spit out both these berries. He guessed it took these alluring berries more out of gentle playfulness rather than any desire to eat. Perhaps this was a happy minor distraction as it rested out of the full force of the river. Perhaps this salmon was in a quite euphoric state of bliss as ancestral memories and dreams of future sensual spawning pleasures mingled in its subconscious mind.

Ian now thought he'd try to take advantage of that salmon's unusual antics. He scrutinized his box of salmon flies. Bright glittering in the Autumnal sunshine, that box's massed display of many coloured gaudy feathers, gold and silver twisted fine wires and gleaming silken threads delighted his searching eyes. Did any of these attractive flies resemble a rowan berry?

He smiled to see an auld *Jock Scott* close embedded with a wanton *Hairy Mary*. Fortunately a *Red Doctor* was embedded nearby if required. He picked up that *Red*

Doctor fly. It boasted a bright red-feathered body that matched the rowan's scarlet brightness.

He tied that fly on. He expertly cast and just avoided getting hooked up on that overhanging rowan branch. The *Red Doctor* swept round and paid an alluring call on that entranced languid salmon. Again it gently rose, again it sucked that 'red berry' down.

The fishing line tightened. The gentle silence ended as the bent rod's madly whirling reel rang out its triumphant scream. The hissing line sliced through the awakened pool in keen pursuit of the rushing salmon.

Ian thrilled in body and soul as his extended nerves put him in direct touch with his primitive pagan ancestors. Near the rocky foot of the pool the large salmon leapt high – a flashing silvery marvel in a glittering sparkle of spray. With experienced skill Ian persuaded his salmon to come back up the agitated pool to him. There was further nerve-testing timeless fishing time when the large salmon again rushed, again leapt high. While all this was going on Ian absolutely forgot all his doubts and worries about Daniel. He even forgot the entire war.

Eventually he landed the defeated salmon.

As he stood admiring the dead salmon's almost fourteen pounds of streamlined silver beauty Daniel joined him. He sincerely congratulated him. He had caught another much smaller salmon. With pleasant leisurely contentment the two successful fishermen soon started out on their return pedestrian journey. Both were very pleased to be carrying the happy extra weight of their fine salmon. It was always great to fairly, sportingly, catch salmon, but it was especially great to have this glorious fresh free food to supplement the meagre and monotonous wartime rations. Neither happy man felt much need for many further words. A companionable contented silence can sometimes be truly golden. Although, as Ian soon discovered, too much silence could all too easily allow all those doubts and damn uncertainties about Daniel to all too actively resurface in his troubled mind.

Ian gave a secret sigh then urged his mind to again drink in the aesthetic wonder of Nature's autumnal beauty. Urged it to marvel with almost sublime delight at seeing the eager rushing Pagan pleasure that the River Tummel surely takes as it journeys from its own loch to join its mighty brother – The Tay.

13

Some weeks after that pleasant fishing trip Ian was once again in his hotel's small office sorting out some guests' surrendered food ration coupons. A tedious task, but one that had to be done. As this war relentlessly continued it brought him more and ever more official forms to be completed in fulfilment of both his hotel and Home Guard duties.

He glanced at his watch and thought, 'Almost six o'clock. Time for the evening news.'

So, almost automatically, he reached out and switched on the office's small wireless.

There was an almost subconscious feeling of grand patriotic British camaraderie in doing this simple thing, as every wireless-owning household in Britain switched on at this important time. It had become a daily ritual.

There was the inevitable patient wait for the wireless valves to warm up. Then a well-known posh English voice came on: 'This is the B.B.C. home service broadcasting from London. Here is the six o'clock news.'

The main news item was the welcome announcement that the American Fifth Army had captured the city of Naples from the retreating Germans. Britain's Eighth Army (the tough, battle-hardened grand old 'Desert Rats') was also relentlessly pushing north in Italy.

Soviet Russia's formidable Red Army (the largest army history has ever seen) after driving the hated Huns from Smolensk, was pushing ever further west in an unstoppable wave of massive fire-power that must, sooner or later, smash on and take Berlin.

As Comrade Stalin, the leader of our grand Soviet Ally, boastfully declared to resounding sycophantic cheers, 'Soon the only German soldiers left in all Russia will be dead German soldiers!'

An outcome all the Allies seemed to wholeheartedly desire (although some had secret deep fears that the Red Army might continue very much further west than defeated Berlin).

Ian welcomed all this encouraging news. After almost three years of war when there had seemed almost nothing but British disasters and defeats it was great that the tide of war had at last turned. It had decisively turned at Stalingrad when the entire German Sixth Army had been surrounded and those Germans who'd survived the Soviet guns and the freezing Russian winter had had to surrender.

From encouraging thoughts of this war's vast canvas, Ian's thoughts once again unapologetically narrowed to a more personal worry, not of fresh news, but rather of a worrying lack of fresh news. It was an unusually long time since his wife and he had received a letter from their son,

Sergeant Andy Gray, who was one of those veteran 'Desert Rats' now serving in the 51st Highland Division 'somewhere in Italy.' Once again he prayed that Andy would survive to rejoice at the final allied victory – whenever that came.

Such worries and prayers again linked him to every household in Britain where anxious parents endlessly waited for, hopefully, reassuring news of sons serving in the Armed Forces.

At least he did not have to worry so much about his two daughters. Both of them, one in the W.A.A.F., the other a nurse, were safely serving within Britain.

The final two items on this evening news seemed almost so familiar that they hardly qualified as news at all. Yet another heavy R.A.F. night-time bombing raid on an already battered German city. Yet another daylight raid by American Flying Fortresses on other important Nazi targets.

Perhaps to the B.B.C those repeated raids were now almost un-newsworthy, but for each R.A.F and American aircrew repeatedly taking part, each raid was a grim matter of dicing with life and a terrible death. For all too many young airmen, dreaded Death all too often won! And those brave allied aircrews were the only ones who, for now, could take the war directly to the guilty German Homeland.

Ian reached out, switched off the wireless and returned his mind to those damn ration coupons. Then with tremendous dramatic suddenness that seeming distant war violently burst in on him.

The office door slammed open. His wife staggered in. She shouted, 'Oh, Ian, Daniel's gone berserk! He's got a gun! He's hit Jeannie!'

Ian jumped up and grasped his trembling wife, 'He's shot her?'

'Oh no. He hit her with it. She's only dazed.'

'Where's Daniel now?'

'Oh God I don't know. He ran away after he hit her.'

'He's run away?' Ian gasped, 'Oh Christ, he's gone after Professor Osborne.'

'Professor Osborne? Oh, Ian, what're you on about?'

'I'll explain later. I must phone John Grant at once.' He eased Anne into the office chair then lifted the phone and instructed 'Auld Maggie,' the old maid in charge of Pitlochry's small manual telephone exchange, to urgently put him through to Police Inspector Grant at the police station or, if not there, at his home,

Despite the seriousness of this matter Ian could not quite resist an inward smile while he impatiently waited to be put through. He knew that 'Auld Maggie' would avidly listen in to this 'urgent' call between him, the Major in command of Pitlochry's Home Guard and Police Inspector Grant. It would be more than her auld blood could stand not to become privy to whatever talk between these important local gentlemen (and officers too!) took place. He must remember to tell the inspector to warn her to keep quiet about whatever she overheard.

Inspector Grant was at his office. Ian gave him the dramatic news about Daniel. 'And

Professor Osborne's at his chalet just now, isn't he?'

'Yes, he is. He only arrived earlier today, as I told you.'

'Oh, John, we better get there before Daniel does.'

'Aye, of course. Ewan's here with me. We'll be there before you.'

'Remember Daniel's got a gun. You better be armed.'

'I've already given Ewan the key to the gun cabinet. We'll both be armed. We'll see you at the professor's chalet.'

Police Sergeant Ewan MacLeod handed a loaded revolver to the inspector then loaded one for himself.

Anne had been listening to Ian's phone call. She asked, 'You're going to the professor's chalet? You think that's where Daniel's going?'

'Yes, we do. I must go there now. I'll get my gun first.'

'Oh God, Ian, be careful. You're too old for such dangerous capers!'

'Oh no I'm not! You know I must do my Home Guard duty.'

'But what's Daniel going to Professor Osborne's for?'

'To kill him!'

'Oh Ian, you're being melodramatic, aren't you?'

'No, I'm not. He's got a gun, hasn't he? Oh, Anne, trust me. I'll explain later. You better get back to Jeanie. Will she need a doctor?'

'No, I don't think so. He didn't hit her too hard. She was slightly stunned and dazed, that's all.'

Ian hurried to their private rooms in the hotel. He opened the cupboard where his Home Guard uniform was hanging. No time to put it on. He grabbed the wide webbing belt with its attached holster. He buckled it on then ran to the garage where he kept his bicycle.

He gave a quick glance at his grand old dark blue Rover car. Oh, if only he'd some petrol that car would take him to the professor's chalet in no time at all.

As he was about to mount his bicycle he thought, 'Oh, I better load my gun in case I meet that bastard Daniel Bailey.'

He withdrew his ·38 Smith &Wesson revolver, took six bullets from the small webbed pouch on his belt and slipped them into the revolver's six chambers. Re-holstering the loaded gun he gave a self-mocking grin, 'Now I'm ready for that treacherous Irish bastard.'

The urgency of his hurry up that slope from the hotel to the A9 road made it feel steeper than ever. With labouring legs and gasping breath he made it to the much flatter main road to Pitlochry.

As he hurried through the silent drowsy wee Perthshire town autumn's thick grey mists merged with dusk's gathering darkness to cloak the small grey houses in a sombre dullness. The sadness of this silent misty misery was greatly compounded by every window being completely blacked-out with not the slightest glimmer of light being allowed to sneak out. Even here in this remote rural backwater 'miles from anywhere' the wartime black-out regulations were strictly enforced.

He soon cycled off the main road and

sped down the slope that took him under the railway bridge. Parked a little further on was Inspector Grant's police car. Ian left his bicycle beside it.

Gasping and panting he toiled up the much steeper slope that led to the Territorial Army armoury and also to Professor Osborne's nearby chalet.

At the top he paused to get his wind back, to peer through the misty dusky half-darkness, to keenly listen for any sound of friend or foe.

Creeping up from the near, but unseen, River Tummel the sombre mists were thicker here and a steady soaking drizzle added an extra misery to the dismal scene.

As Ian made cautious progress towards the blacked-out dark chalet with his revolver held ready the mists and drizzle increased their shrouding grip on sodden shrubs and shivery trees.

Silent, motionless, he stood by a tree and peered all around. His gaze focused on one place. Was that a cowering shrub or a crouching man?

The longer he stared the more it seemed that that man – or shrub – was alive with vague motion. Remembering an army sniper's and a Highland deerstalker's wise advice he looked away for a short time then returned his refreshed gaze to that place.

Yes, that misty vague shape really was only an innocent shrub. But how easily that armed menace, Daniel Bailey, could be lurking somewhere amongst that confusion of dusk, mist and miserable drizzle.

He swivelled around with revolver pointing as a figure appeared from the darkness.

With relief he lowered his gun and smiled a greeting as he recognised his friend, Inspector John Grant.

'What's happening, John?' he whispered.

'Nothing so far. There's no sign of Daniel Bailey. I've warned the professor to stay locked in his chalet and not to open it to anyone but you, Ewan or myself.'

'Where is Ewan?'

'He's keeping guard at the west end of the chalet. I'll go back and hide in these trees.

You better keep watch near the east end of the chalet.'

Ian followed these whispered instructions and so, hidden from each other, but happy in the knowledge that their alert armed friends were near, those three men silently waited.

They did not have too long to wait.

With startling suddenness two loud shots rang out.

To Ian and John they seemed to come from near the far end of the chalet. That was where Police Sergeant Ewan MacLeod was stationed. Had he fired these shots? Or had they been fired at him by Daniel? Did Ewan need their help? Should they cautiously move towards him to find out what had happened? Or should they stay where they were and continue to guard the professor in his chalet?

Those questions were soon answered as three rapid shots blasted out. Then three more shots were quickly added. All came from near the west end of the chalet.

As the Police Inspector and the Home Guard commander stood anxiously staring into the concealing misty drizzle with revolvers held ready they were relieved to hear the bulky police sergeant's distinctive Highland voice shout out, 'Och, everything's all right now, Inspector. I've shot that bastard. I think he's dead!'

Daniel Bailey was lying flat on his back. Both arms were flung straight out.

Inspector Grant knelt at one side of him. Major Gray knelt at the other side. Both tried to find a pulse. Both failed. The inspector said, 'He's gone, Ian.'

Ian nodded in solemn agreement, 'Aye, John, there's no doubt about that.'

John shone his torch in Daniel's wide open eyes. They had already dulled to the awful blankness of death. He gently closed the eyelids. He opened up Daniel's blood stained jacket. The torch's searching beam disclosed his shirt to be a soggy mess of blood that still almost seemed to flow from many bullet wounds in his deep chest and concave abdomen.

John stared at Ian and quietly said, 'There must be three or four, or even more bullets there.'

Ian again nodded his agreement, 'Aye, obviously Ewan was making sure he killed him.'

'Aye, he well and truly made sure o' that all right.'

Both men rose, brushed damp grass from wet trouser knees, then stood beside the police sergeant who had been silently standing and looking on.

'Well, Ewan,' John said, 'you certainly made sure that that treacherous bastard died. You emptied your entire revolver into him, didn't you?'

Seeming to come out of a trance, Ewan gasped, 'What.....? What.....? Oh aye, but at first I only gave him three bullets. Then I saw that he was a bastard wee Jap, so I gave him the other three.'

With instant mutual empathy John and Ian exchanged understanding glances. Obviously poor Ewan had killed that 'Jap' to avenge his son, Colin, who had been killed by Japanese soldiers in Burma a few months ago.

Ewan now seemed to return to being a rational police sergeant presenting his official report. 'That Daniel was the first to start shooting. He fired two shots at me. In the obscuring mist they both missed. Then he an' me played a deadly game o' hide and seek through a' the misty drizzle and ghostly shrubs an' trees. Then I saw him first. And I shot him first.'

'Aye, you did well, Ewan, you really did.' John said. Ian added his agreement, 'Aye, Ewan, you did what we would have tried to do in your place.'

After a thoughtful pause John said, 'I suppose that, seeing the chalet being well-guarded by us, Daniel realised he wouldn't be able to kill the professor, so perhaps he decided to try to kill a British policeman instead.'

The three men fell silent. They stood in a solemn group staring down at that shot corpse.

What an insignificant small thing it now seemed. In dusk's thickening darkness and the misty drizzle's vague dimness that dead body seemed little more than an obscure dark mound on the sodden ground. A valueless thing that could easily merge with the surrounding mud. Where were all its hopes of glory? Where were all its wild "sound and fury" now?

These three men looked on not with cold indifference, but with calm acceptance. They had all come through the awfulness of the First World War. They had seen many good comrades savagely die. They had seen – and smelled – the obscene horrors of lost soldiers' decomposing bodies. So the violent death of one more man did not seem all that much to them. Especially not when the man killed had been a deceiving treacherous enemy. A man who deserved to die.

Their silence dramatically ended when they heard a British Army sentry's traditional challenge being shouted: 'Halt! Halt or I fire! Who goes there? Friend or Foe?'

Recognising that aged and somewhat quavery voice, Ian shouted, 'Is that you, Sandy?'

'Aye, it is. Is that you, Major Gray?'

'Aye, it is.' Ian echoed.

'Did you do a' yon shooting?'

'Yes we did. But everything's under control now, Sandy. And I assure you we're your friends, not your foes!'

As he came stumbling and grumbling towards them through the misty gloom they all saw that he truly was Auld Sandy Robertson, the veteran Home Guard corporal who was caretaker at the nearby Territorial Army armoury. With grave misgivings they also saw that he was pointing a Sten sub-machine gun vaguely in their direction.

'Oh, Sandy,' Ian urgently shouted, 'don't point that damn gun at us!'

'Oh no, of course not. I'm sorry Major. But don't panic, sir, it is loaded, but the safety catch is on.' To prove this he fingered the trigger. A blast of bullets sped to the left of where the three men had been standing. They were now all lying flat on the ground. A hail of swearing and curses assaulted poor, confused Auld Sandy.

After Ian had taken the Sten gun from an almost weepingly contrite Sandy, his unintended targets relented.

'Och, Sandy, we ken you were only trying to do your duty,' Ewan forgivingly said. The other two generously agreed.

Then Ian grinned, 'Oh, Sandy, you didn't really think we were not your good old friends but your nasty Nazi foes, did you?'

Smiling his relief and thanks Auld Sandy said, 'Och no, Major, I didn't. I was damned sure the safety catch was correctly on. Och nae doot I'm getting too auld for even my easy Home Guard duties.'

'Och no you're not, Sandy,' Ewan said. Then, thinking of his 'Jap' illusion, added with a wide grin, 'We can all make damn silly mistakes.'

There were more smiles and grins then, pleased to see the tension eased, Inspector Grant now took control. 'I'll go to the armoury with you, Sandy, to use your phone. I must let Special Branch in Glasgow know what's happened to Daniel. And, Ian, would you let Professor Osborne know that he's quite safe now. He must be wondering what the hell all the shooting was about. Oh, and Ewan do you mind waiting here by the

corpse until Ian and I come back? We won't
be long.'

When John came back he found Ian waiting
with Ewan by Daniel's stiff corpse. Ian
informed him that, to show his thanks for
their protecting him, Professor Osborne
had invited them in for "a drink." 'Although
I don't know if he means merely tea or
something stronger.'

'I hope tae God he means a dram,' Ewan
said.

Ian laughed, 'Spoken like a true West
Highlander, Ewan.'

John unfolded the combined army
groundsheet and camouflaged rainproof
cape he was carrying. He explained, 'I
thought Special Branch might want us to
leave Daniel's body at 'the site of the crime'
until they arrive tomorrow. But they told me
in no uncertain terms that such peacetime
niceties did not apply in this wartime case
of vile treachery. We must get his body

somewhere out of sight and hush up his drastic death as much as possible.'

'So we'll carry him on this cape and hide him in Auld Sandy's T.A. Armoury.'

This they did and in that secure small armoury with its iron-barred window and double locked internal door the familiar smell of gun oil disguised the uglier smell of blood and fresh death.

Leaving Sandy cleaning his unloaded Sten gun, (he'd double checked!) and telling him to say nothing about this death and to tell anyone who enquired about all that dusk shooting that it had only been some limited Home Guard semi-darkness practice, the other three made their eager way to Professor Osborne's chalet.

Once they were ushered in, Ewan's delighted gaze alighted on a bottle of Glenlivet malt whisky and four crystal tumblers. His eyes sparkled – his silent prayer answered!

Ian had never been in this chalet. He looked around with keen interest. From floor to ceiling two walls were all bookcases.

Every shelf was tightly crowded. He glanced at some of the bright titles. There were many volumes on a vast variety of scientific subjects. These were biographies of, and works by Galileo, Newton, Darwin and our own time's outstanding genius, the still living, still profoundly thinking, Einstein. A most impressive list.

There were shelves of Science Fiction. Many volumes by H. G. Wells with his seeming fantastic predictions that were now, or were becoming, most unpleasant facts. The deadly attacks by fleets of bombing aircraft, the development of long range rockets, the constant threats of the use of poison gas or even anthrax (Ian knew of anthrax's secretly practised use near Ewan's old West Highland home beside Gruinard Island)

There were novels by Jules Verne and more recent, more fantastic S.F. authors. Then Ian was delighted to see many of his own favourite novels by the greatest 19th century authors – Dickens, Tolstoy and Balzac. He also eagerly greeted a large collection of the greatest short story author of all – Somerset Maugham. Obviously this scientific professor was very well read, was an all-round cultured man.

This was further confirmed by an impressive large oil painting, a seascape sunset, the sky alive with a Turnerish glow of golden glowing yellows and bright blushing pinks.

Ian was further impressed when he noticed a framed black and white photo of Professor Osborne and another white-coated scientist standing beside Winston Churchill in some laboratory. For once the Prime Minister was not holding or smoking a large Havana cigar.

He wondered if that laboratory was where the professor was doing some ultra-secret, ultra-sensitive scientific research that was so delicate that even good old cigar-loving Winston was not allowed to smoke.

Soon the professor and his three delighted guests were sitting in comfort with a generous tumbler of malt whisky lovingly grasped in their caressing hands.

With what seemed a nervous grin the professor explained his possession of this very rare, very precious wartime treasure. 'Oh, please don't you gentlemen think that I drink like this often. I assure you I don't.' He aimed another grin at the police inspector and police sergeant, 'And I assure you two sturdy bastions of the law that I didn't buy this bottle of whisky on the illegal Black Market.'

His uncertain grin transformed into decidedly eccentric giggly laughter. He seemed vastly amused by his attempt at a joke. His guests joined in with more robust and straightforward laughter. Were they laughing more at him, than with him? But as they politely laughed they wondered, 'When the hell is he going to lift his glass and drink? We're dying to join in with him in the glorious business of drinking, not merely bloody laughing.'

But the teasing professor was in no hurry. He still did not raise his golden glowing tumbler. Instead he explained, 'I don't mean to boast, you know, but I got this special whisky as a special perquisite in acknowledgement of some very difficult secret scientific work I'd successfully done.'

At last he raised his glass, gave the Gaelic toast,' Slainte Mhath!' then drank.

His three guests followed his belated example with eager speed.

In a pleasant atmosphere of glowing satisfied sighs Ian asked, 'Are you staying long this time, professor? Will you have time for a day's salmon fishing?'

'Oh I'm afraid not. I must return down south in two days' time, more's the pity. I'll only manage short morning walks to drink in the glorious Perthshire autumnal scenes.' He fell into a sudden strange staring silence.

His puzzled guests stared at him and waited for him to continue. But he seemed in some strange deep trance.

How could his three welcome guests – all fine men, but without deep scientific minds – possibly guess at how, when he was on his carefree and absent-minded seeming, morning strolls through Keats glorious season of mists and mellow fruitfulness, he could never be entirely free from tortuous thoughts, doubts and worries in his over-active brain about his top secret, vitally important scientific work?

How could these scientifically innocent men ever guess that scientists such as he, held the future of mankind in the palms of their trembling hands?

He was helping to develop a fantastic ultra-secret weapon that would win the war for the Allies or might destroy all mankind!

Our British and American scientists had to perfect this new weapon before formidable German scientific brains perfected it first. The thought of these Nazis being able to win this war for Hitler was unimaginably appalling!

With a violent start Professor Osborne came out of his trance. He stammered a grinning apology. He pointed to his paper-laden desk, 'Even when here on a short holiday I must do lots of urgent "homework".'

When looking at the professor's books Ian had noticed that desk. He'd even tried to read some of the many sheets of paper neatly stacked on it. He'd hoped they might give a clue to what secret work he was engaged in. But every sheet was face down.

He was impressed by this example of the professor's neat security habits. They were in unexpected sharp contrast to his rather bohemian appearance, his almost ragged careless clothes, his rather long, untidy, rarely combed greying hair.

John now said, 'Oh, professor, could you please be sure to be in tomorrow afternoon? The Special Branch detectives from Glasgow will want to interview you.'

'Oh yes, of course.' He again strangely grinned, again erratically laughed, again pointed to his laden desk, 'I'll be chained to my inescapable work there.'

After draining his tumbler John got to his feet, 'We better get back to our wives. They'll be worried about us. Oh and now that Daniel's dead you should be safe enough now, you've always got Auld Sandy at the armoury to keep discreet guard over you if thought necessary.'

The whisky flush on Ewan's glowing face seemed to give him temporary ease from his deep etched grief over the death of his son, so as he stood up he smiled and asked, 'Aye, but who's going tae protect the professor from Auld Sandy's rather erratic, rather dangerous guarding habits?'

14

Detective Inspector Harry Brown and Detective Sergeant Tom Kerr from Glasgow's Special Branch stood staring down at Daniel Bailey's dead body lying on its camouflaged army cape in Pitlochry's Territorial Army armoury.

Police Inspector John Grant also stood silently looking on from behind the two counter-espionage experts.

Auld Sandy Robertson hovered somewhere further back in the drill hall. He was smartly dressed in his Home Guard corporal's uniform. His double row of campaign ribbons made a bright proud show on his khaki tunic. He lingered in the hope of receiving more orders, of being, or seeming to be, of real use to those police officers.

The Detective Inspector gave a twisted grin, 'Your Sergeant MacLeod really made sure he'd kill him, didn't he? He made a damned good job of executing that bastard Irish traitor.'

'Aye, he certainly did,' Inspector Grant agreed. He thought it best to say no more. He very well knew that even in the midst of this desperate war against Nazi evil, Glasgow's Special Branch were still deeply involved in keeping discreet watch on shadowy activities by both Catholic and Protestant fanatics.

'Is that Bailey's gun over there?' Brown asked.

'Aye, it is,' John lifted it from a shelf and handed it to the Detective Inspector with a warning, 'Be careful, Inspector, it's still loaded.'

Brown again grinned, 'Och, it's all right. I've handled guns before, you know. And there's no need to worry about our fingerprints on it, is there? We're not investigating a murder. We're merely checking up on and reporting on a fully justified wartime death. A killing that carries no guilt, that was as necessary as is a British soldier's killing of his German enemies.'

After inspecting the gun, Brown handed it over to Detective Sergeant Kerr, 'What do you make of this weapon, Tom?'

'Well obviously it's a ·38 Smith &Wesson revolver, a standard British Army Officer's sidearm. Two bullets have been fired from it recently. Another four bullets are still loaded in it.' He peered at the revolver more closely, 'But here's the most interesting thing. Its maker's serial number has been neatly filed away.'

Brown nodded, 'Aye, exactly. We both know what that means, don't we?' The Special Branch Detective Inspector and Detective Sergeant exchanged meaningful glances. Both suspected that violent means might have been used to transfer that revolver from a British Army Officer to some dangerously hostile Irish hands.

Brown turned to Inspector Grant, 'We'll take this body and this gun back to Glasgow with us. And of course we'll take Bailey's radio transmitter too. Then Tom and I will be kept busy trying to check up on these three items. So, Inspector, you better now guide us to the Glen Hotel. We'll collect that transmitter and interview some people there.'

At the hotel Inspector Grant introduced the two detectives to its owners, Ian Gray and his wife, Anne. Speaking in his role as the fully involved local Home Guard commander, Ian confirmed every detail of the Inspector's police report on the guarding of professor Osborne, the hunt for and shooting dead of their ex-hotel chef, Daniel Bailey.

Anne now told of Jeannie, their hotel's young maid of all work, and her important part in this dramatic story. 'The poor wee innocent lass is terribly shaken by Bailey's attack on her and by the astounding revelation that that Irishman whom she thought of as quite a friend was all the time a deceiving evil monster. Was a vile traitor not only to her and all of us at the hotel, but also in effect to her much loved older brothers, one a 'Desert Rat' serving 'somewhere in Italy', the other a member of that elite group, the Lovat Scouts, engaged in Commando-like secret missions.'

'So anyway, I told the tearful lass to stay in bed and rest all day. But if you do need to interview her she said she'd get up and speak to you.'

The Detective Inspector compassionately said, 'Och, I don't think there's any need for us to disturb the poor lass. What do you think, Tom?'

'Och no, sir, I'm sure Mrs Gray can confirm all the information we already have.'

Brown nodded, 'Aye, that's true. Now, Mrs Gray, would you please tell us exactly what happened to wee Jeannie.'

This she eagerly did. 'When working as a chamber-maid Jeannie heard Daniel Bailey seemingly talking to himself in his quite secluded staff bedroom. Thinking it would be amusing to catch him foolishly talking to himself, she knocked on his door then entered his bedroom with her face beaming ready smiles.

'She did not see him but heard his voice coming from the attic above his bedroom. Puzzled, she shouted up at him.

'He came storming down the steep ladder from the attic where he'd been talking on his secret German radio transmitter. He hit her with his gun and stunned her. He then ran away.

'Then, as we all now know, he made his way to Professor Osborne's chalet intending to carry out his orders to kill him.'

'Thank you, Mrs Gray. That exactly confirms Inspector Grant's report. Oh and how is poor wee Jeannie's injured head now?'

'Oh it's not too bad. Some bruising and quite swollen, but she's not in too much pain, thank God.'

'Good! I'm delighted to hear it. Now Tom and I will go up and collect that traitor's radio transmitter. We'll also search his bedroom and take away anything of interest.'

'I'll guide you to his room,' Ian suggested, 'there's quite a confusing maze of staff bedrooms up there,'

'Thank you. Oh, and Mrs Gray, would it be possible for Tom and me to have a light snack? We've had nothing to eat since breakfast.'

'Oh surely. That's no bother. How would a bowl of my thick Scotch Broth and some bacon sandwiches do?'

'They'd be great. Thank you.'

After placing the radio transmitter and Bailey's bulging suitcase in their police car, the two Glasgow detectives did full justice to Anne's effortlessly provided snack. Grinning she asked, 'Would you two prefer tea or this "coffee"?' She held up a bottle full of thick dark liquid. It was grandly labelled Supreme Dandelion Coffee.'

The detectives simultaneously exclaimed, 'Oh, the tea for me, please.'

Anne laughed, 'Obviously, like me, you don't care for this unique Supreme Coffee.' She gave a reminiscent sigh, 'Oh, it must be more than three years since I last tasted real coffee.'

Ian also laughed, 'Och, Anne, I'm sure these gentlemen will be fine once they've got mugs o' good strong char.'

So the two detectives soon stood, both with a mug of char in one hand and a cigarette in the other. Gazing out of the hotel's lounge windows they admired the fine pastoral views that stretched to an almost hidden river then rose to a tree clad ridge. The varied trees glowed their varied shades of autumnal glory.

'What river is that?' Brown asked Ian.

'Oh, that's the Tummel.'

'Oh, the Tummel. A fine salmon river, I believe.'

'Aye it is. The hotel has a beat on it. I enjoy good fishing there at its three grand salmon pools.'

'In Inspector Grant's report I noticed that Bailey also liked fishing there.'

'Aye, he did. But only very occasionally when hotel guests had not booked the fishing.'

'I see,' Brown thoughtfully paused then asked, 'And was Bailey a good fisher?'

'Oh yes, he was a very skilled fisherman. That was obvious the first time I saw him fishing.'

Brown again paused then rather mysteriously said, 'That's very interesting that he was a good salmon fisherman.'

Ian gazed questioningly at him, but the Special Branch detective revealed no further hints of his hidden thoughts.

Brown glanced at his watch and grinned at Ian, 'I would like to have a quick look at your three salmon pools. It's not just because Tom and I are also quite keen fishermen, but it's also to do with Bailey's death.'

Detective Sergeant Tom Kerr smiled widely. 'Aye, sir, it'll be grand to stretch our legs and get a breath o' fresh air before we drive back to the miseries o' Glasgow's filthy black smoky fog.' He said no more, but he correctly guessed at the hidden thinking behind his superior officer's desire to see that river and inspect the hotel's three pools.

More mystified than ever, Ian agreed to Brown's request, 'Oh of course I'll take you there. It's always pleasant to stroll by the river even when not fishing. At this time of year when the hen salmon are heavy with spawn we cease fishing and leave them in peace,'

For those three men it really was most pleasant to go along the track that led down from the Glen Hotel to the attractive River Tummel.

The fields they passed were crowded with cattle or sheep. As in all British farms every possible acre was in full productive use to help feed the severely rationed Nation and reduce the amount of food that had to be shipped in by these unsung heroes, the British Merchant Seamen who, convoy after convoy, defied the grim dangers of packs of ruthless German U-boats.

Arriving at the first pool, Ian said, 'This is the Grey Rock Pool.' He grinned and pointed at the large grey rock that jutted up at the foot of the pool, 'No mystery about how it got that name.'

The next pool's name was more obscure. 'This is the Bull Pool,' Ian then quickly explained before the detectives asked the obvious question. 'Seemingly a large rogue bull was accidentally drowned here sometime in early Victorian times.'

The two detectives exchanged meaningful glances that Ian could not understand. How could he guess at the deceptive 'bullshit' they had in mind for this most appropriately named pool?

The third pool was the largest and the most attractive. 'This is the Glen Pool,' Ian said. 'Although some auld ghillies used to call it the Green Park Pool. No one knows why it changed its name. There used to be a fishers' cabin here and Shetland ponies were kept in that adjoining field where well-brought up Victorian children could happily ride and be seen but not heard.'

'Aye, it's a real braw pool,' the two detectives agreed. Then again the exchange of that meaningful glance.

Brown said, 'Thank you, Ian, this has been most interesting for us, not only seeing this river, these pools, as keen fishermen, but also seeing them as Special Branch detectives too.'

Once more Ian was mystified. Brown saw this, he smiled, but tantalisingly said no more.

Ian was getting annoyed at being kept in the dark. Surely as a Home Guard major these special policemen could confide in him. Then, remembering the Careless Talk posters and the Intelligence Service's need to know principle he relented. No doubt he would hear what this excursion to the River Tummel was all about in due course. Or would he?

The three men returned to the hotel then got into the police car. As he drove, Brown explained, 'Inspector Grant returned to Pitlochry's police station after he guided us here. Now he should be waiting for us at Professor Osborne's chalet, Sergeant MacLeod should be with him.'

They were. Inspector Grant introduced the two Special Branch detectives to the professor. Ian also shook his hand. In fact there was an all round shaking of hands. Perhaps they were congratulatory handshakes on them having executed that traitor, Bailey, and having successfully guarded the most important professor.

All six smiling men felt themselves enwrapped in a warm fraternal glow. A feeling of war-engendered camaraderie at a good job well done.

For the four policemen, two in uniform, two in civvies, perhaps there was an extra fraternal glow, a deep proud brotherhood from them all serving in the police force and all having given strong, warm and correct handshakes.

As they all stood talking, Ian noted how the trained observant eyes of both detectives took in this large, book-lined room. He saw them once again exchange a meaningful glance as they saw that framed picture of Professor Osborne standing beside Winston Churchill in what must surely be some top-secret laboratory. No doubt they too were pleased to see this proof of just how important a scientist this professor must be. Important enough to justify a man being shot dead to keep him safe.

Then with a burst of sudden energy the professor started moving chairs about while hospitably urging, 'Be seated, gentlemen. Please be seated.'

As his five guests got themselves sorted out, the professor apologised, 'I'm such a poor host. I haven't any whisky left to offer you. But what about tea? Would you like some?'

All his guests rejected this suggestion, 'Oh, no thanks. We've just had some... We're fine as we are.'

The professor ran nervous fingers through his unruly long hair and gave his shrill giggly laugh, 'Oh, it's just as well you don't want any tea. I don't think I've got more than one cup and one chipped mug and I've got no saucers at all!'

His guests joined in with their louder, deeper, more manly laughter. They all had the same thoughts: that great scientific and intellectual minds often came with strange eccentricities or what sometimes seemed damned near to outright madness.

Detective Inspector Brown now took control, 'Well, gentlemen, let's get down to official business. I've been ordered by my Top Brass to keep this shooting dead of Bailey a deep secret. Because of him being an Irishman from Dublin in the neutral Irish

Republic and possibly having links to Belfast and even to Glasgow, apart from his radio transmitter links direct to some German controller, we have to treat this event with extreme caution. We've to handle it with velvet gloves, in fact. But before I get on to our official cover story I've a question for you, Ewan.'

Pleased to hear the Detective Inspector use his Christian name, Police Sergeant Ewan Macleod smiled and said, 'I'll willingly answer any question, sir.'

'Thank you. It's just that I'm rather surprised that you fired all six of your revolver bullets into Bailey. Wasn't that somewhat excessive?'

Ewan seemed greatly confused. He stammered, 'Oh I... I only gave him three bullets at first. Then vaguely seeing the huddled wee bastard I thought he was a lurking Jap, so I gave him the other three!'

The detective inspector was puzzled. 'You thought him a Jap? A Japanese soldier here in Pitlochry in 1943? Surely that was most unlikely?'

'Oh, I agree now it seems damned stupid.' Ewan again seemed very confused, 'But... then he really did look like a bloody skulking Jap!'

As the detective inspector continued his puzzled stare, Inspector Grant spoke up for his sergeant. 'Perhaps I could explain, inspector?'

'Yes, please do, John.'

Also pleased by the use of his Christian name, John explained, 'Ewan's son – his only son – Colin, was killed by Japanese soldiers when fighting in Burma with the British 14th Army, The Forgotten Army, about three months ago. By shooting that 'Jap' Ewan was trying to avenge the death of his only son.'

'Oh, I see. Oh, now I understand. I'm very sorry for your son's death, Ewan.' Detective Inspector Brown paused, he sighed, 'I know how you feel, Ewan. Our son's fairly recent death is a heavy burden my wife and I have to carry too.'

'Was your son also in the Army?'

'Oh, no. No, he was a Merchant Navy officer on a large oil tanker. They were sunk by a U-boat. There were no survivors.'

There was a solemn silence. The most imaginative of the sympathetic listeners all too vividly pictured Brown's son's tragic death. They almost saw that thick layer of black oil coating and calming the sea's surface. Saw it blinding the struggling sailors' eyes, filling their mouths, choking their throats and clogging their lungs. A monstrous death! But, sadly, only one of the many hideous ways humans have devised for other humans to die in this 'greatest' of all wars.

Brown again sighed. Again said, 'Now, gentlemen, let's get back to our official business. As I've already told you this shooting dead of that traitor, Bailey, has to be kept secret. In fact officially it never happened.

'What did happen was that that keen fisher, Bailey, met an accidental death when fishing the Bull Pool on the Glen Hotel's beat on the River Tummel. He must have fallen in. His drowned body was found at the next pool, the Glen Pool.

'His drowning was simply one more unfortunate accidental fishing death. That's the cover story we will all stick to. You all agree?'

All nodded their wholehearted agreement. Ian Gray smiled at Brown, 'That's why you were so keen to see the River Tummel and my hotel's salmon pools.'

Brown returned his smile, 'Aye, it was. Oh, but I assure you Tom and I really are quite keen fishermen too. Perhaps after this bloody long war is finished we might manage a day's fishing in these pools.'

'Oh, of course, I'll easily arrange that. You will be welcome guests.'

Inspector Grant now asked, 'What about the noise of all the shots at Bailey's killing? Do you have a cover story for them as well?'

'No, I've nothing quite so definite.' Brown now addressed Ian, 'As the Home Guard commander, you must now order your men not to enquire too deeply into all that shooting. Perhaps you best say that the Police Inspector, the Sergeant and you were just having some target practice to see how accurate you could be in dusk's confusing dimness. I think that should be cover enough, don't you?'

'Yes, I agree. That should do fine.'

Professor Osborne now somewhat hesitantly spoke up, 'Oh, but what about Auld Sandy Robertson? You know how he did his best to guard me. Mightn't he inadvertently let slip what all the shooting was about?'

Ian grinned his reply, 'Oh I very much doot if any enquirer will be able to make much sense of Auld Sandy's replies. When Sandy gets going with his stories the enquirer won't know if he's hearing about German paratroops (some disguised as nuns!) being dropped near Pitlochry; about capturing Hun soldiers in their Flanders trenches in the last war, or even if he's away back in Sandy's Great Boring Stories about the Boer War.'

After the general laughter, Brown glanced at his watch then said, 'Tom and I will take Bailey's drowned body, his gun, radio transmitter and all his other gear back to Glasgow now. The pathologist will confirm he died of drowning. Bailey's next of kin in Dublin will be informed of his unfortunate accidental death. His body will be quickly cremated. If requested, his ashes will be sent to his relations. ' He paused and enquiringly glanced around, 'I think that about covers everything, gentlemen. Unless any of you have any questions?'

Four of the men shook their heads. The fifth seemed more unsure. 'Do you have some doubts about all this, professor?' Brown asked.

'Oh what ....? Oh no .... Oh no... not at all. But it's just a disturbing thought that when the pathologist carries out his autopsy on Bailey's drowned body won't he be somewhat mystified at all the bullet wounds in that drowned cadaver?'

Brown gave a half grin, 'Aye, no doubt will. But he – like us in the police and Home Guard – will do what he's told to do. He will obey all orders coming down from the mighty Higher Powers. That pathologist will, again like us, have signed the Official Secrets Act. I don't know if these wartime constraints apply to you, professor?'

'Oh they do, inspector.' He again gave his strange shrill laugh, 'Oh I assure you they most certainly do! In fact the forms I signed to do with my security clearance were much more strict and stringent than your mere Official Secrets Act. Although actually I signed that too. So yes, I agree the would-be assassin, Bailey, had an accidental drowning death and, as far as I know, there were absolutely no bullets in his drowned body.'

'Good. Good. So now we're all agreed on that.'

Inspector Grant again spoke up, 'I'm sorry to keep you back, Detective Inspector, but I remember from your confidential Special Branch report that Bailey had two brothers serving in the British Army. If they were upset by his death and, not knowing he was a traitor, one of them came to see where he'd drowned we would all need to be extra vigilant not to let him suspect there was anything in the least suspicious about his brother's death, won't we?'

'Yes, you would. A good point, John. I'm glad you raised it.' Brown now addressed Ian

Gray, 'If one of Bailey's brothers does visit you at your hotel and wants to see where his brother drowned you could handle that all right, couldn't you Ian?'

'Oh yes. Certainly. I'll instruct all at the hotel to strictly keep to our cover story about Bailey's unfortunate death. If requested, I'll take his brother to see the pool where Daniel Bailey drowned.'

'Good. Now that's all in order.' Brown paused, he seemed to have finished, then he decided to say some more. 'If Bailey's brothers ever discovered he'd not been accidentally drowned, but had been shot dead by the British Police, their reactions might well be rather wild and drastic. They could cause us a lot of most unpleasant trouble.' He paused, he deeply sighed, 'Oh Tom and I are all too well aware of how terribly sensitive anything connected with the Irish and their long and ugly history of both Catholic and Protestant bigotry and hatred are. We always try to be most careful not to do anything that might fan these ever smouldering hatreds into full, fierce, tragic flames.' There was a thoughtful silence. It was broken by Professor Osborne's strangely agitated voice, 'Oh yes, we all know how terrible are history's religious bigots. It's enough to make us despair of all mankind. Oh I and my fellow scientists used to think that our good pure science would cure all, or most of, mankind's terrible ills. But now this bloody war has made us almost as guilty as any religious fanatic. We're ceaselessly devising ever 'better' things to ever more hideously kill ever more humans, both the vile guilty and the tragic innocent.'

He knew he shouldn't, but Brown could not resist asking, 'What science are you involved in, professor?'

The professor again gave his strange shrill laugh, 'Oh my dear Detective Inspector, you know you shouldn't ask me that, The Official Secrets Act, the dangers of Careless Talk, the need to know principle and all that, you know.'

The others tried to hide their smiles at Brown's obvious annoyed discomfort.

The professor also saw his annoyance and contritely apologised, 'Oh I'm sorry, my dear Brown, I didn't mean to annoy you. Of course I know that you and all of us here are completely trustworthy. All of us hate the Horrid Huns and the Nasty Nazis, don't we?'

Inspector Grant replied for them all, 'Yes, of course we do.' He cast a sympathetic eye at Brown whose son had been killed by a German U-boat's torpedo, then at Ewan MacLeod whose only son had been killed by the Germans eastern ally, the Japanese. 'Two of our friends here have profound reasons to deeply hate the vile Germans and the obnoxious Japs, haven't they?'

With ready empathy the professor agreed, 'Yes, of course they do. We all deeply sympathise with you, Brown, and you, MacLeod, over the sad loss of your brave young sons.'

These two bereaved men nodded their thanks for this true sympathy, true friendship.

Moved by the palpable atmosphere of shared sorrows and fine patriotic friendship, Professor Osborne withdrew the cloak of secrecy that shrouded his vital scientific work. 'Oh surely I'm doing nothing wrong in telling you good friends that I'm engaged in the rather obscure science of Theoretical Nuclear Physics.'

He again trilled his strange shrill laugh, 'Oh I see from all your uncomprehending blank faces that my fantastic science means nothing to any of you gentlemen.'

'No, it certainly doesn't,' they all agreed.

'Well I can tell you this much, gentleman: some of the greatest British and American scientists (and I'm not including myself in that description!) are urgently engaged in developing an entirely new type of weapon. Something the likes of which the world has never seen before. Top German scientists are trying to develop this secret weapon too. We're all engaged in a frenzied race to be first to create this fantastic new secret weapon... Whoever wins this race will also win this war!'

The professor paused and gazed around at the astounded faces. 'Oh, I'm sorry, my good friends, I've said much more than I should have. All this is, of course, top secret, you know.'

'Yes, of course we'll all keep this amazing knowledge a deep secret,' Inspector Grant said. 'But if I might ask just one question? Is this desperate scientific race the reason why Daniel Bailey tried to kill you?'

'Yes, it is. I was warned to be careful. Our Secret Service ordered Special Branch to protect all our scientists, including humble wee me (again that crazy laugh) from possible German assassins.' He beamed at Sergeant MacLeod, 'Thanks to your bravery and sharp shooting, Ewan, my life was saved and my would-be assassin shot dead.'

Ewan grinned, 'Oh no he wasn't! Officially he accidently drowned, remember?' Then, perhaps for the first time since his son's death, Ewan gave an outright laugh, 'The only one I shot then was yon bloody lurking bastard Jap!'

Once the understanding sympathetic laughter died down a grinning Ian Gray said, 'That was a typical dastardly Nazi thing to do – to try to kill you, professor.'

'Yes, of course it was. Just what you'd expect from these Nasty Nazis.' He burst into his unique laugh, 'Oh but no doubt our brave, noble, British Special Agents are also trying to kill German scientists engaged in this vital project. But that's quite a different story, isn't it?'

Brown laughed then said, 'Oh well now, professor, if you've no more interesting secrets to reveal, I'll get on with loading Bailey's drowned body into the police car.'

'Actually there is one more thing I must tell you all. In a few days' time I'm returning to my secret work 'somewhere in England', then, if all goes to plan, I'll be on my way to the good old U.S.A.'

'Oh really? That'll be exciting for you, professor,' Brown said. Then again he asked a question he knew he shouldn't, 'Will you still be engaged in this vital secret race over there?'

'Yes, I most certainly shall. With their vast resources and ample empty space to test their unique new secret weapon, the Americans are – we all fervently hope – in the lead in this desperate race. However some British scientists, including me, I'm pleased to say, are going to work with them and help them achieve their decisive goal before Germany's most brilliant scientists do.'

There was a tense silence as the five keen listening un-scientific men tried to take in and understand all this alarming new knowledge they had acquired. Had acquired when they shouldn't have. Surely Professor Osborne would be in deep trouble if the Powers-That-Be discovered he'd broken the Official Secrets Act by telling them what they shouldn't know.

Despite that worrying thought, Ian Gray could not resist asking one more question, 'If this fantastic new secret weapon is as war-winningly powerful as you think it will be, surely to God there's no real danger of the Germans getting it first, is there?'

'Oh I hope to God there's not! But anyone who knows just how many brilliant scientists and engineers the Germans have must he deeply worried.' After giving what seemed a more shrill and more nervous laugh, the professor urgently added, 'So if any of you fine men believe in the power of prayer (which, being a scientific atheist, I do not) I urge you to pray with your utmost might that your God really is on our side.'

All knew this subject was now closed.

All these men crowded into Professor Osborne's book-lined study felt darkly burdened by this worrying secret knowledge that they must never share with anyone else.

Detective Inspector Brown got to his feet and said, 'Right, gentlemen, let's have no more delay. Let's load Bailey's drowned body. Then Tom and I will be on our way. All of you please remember that there was no such thing as any shooting of any Irish traitor, all right?'

They nodded their agreement.

As he left the professor's chalet Ian Gray had the final word. He grinned and said, 'I suppose we could call this event that officially never happened, *Pitlochry's Secret War*, couldn't we?'

Before getting off to sleep that night Ian and Anne Gray once again talked over yesterday's, and today's most interesting events. Ian really appreciated his wife's thoughtful forbearance in not gloating over this latest proof of the reality of her deep intuitive powers that had warned her of Daniel Bailey's possible untrustworthy and deceptive character.

Anne had merely said, 'Well, Ian, you must admit that my strongly felt but well concealed distrust of that deceiving rotter, Bailey, was fully justified, wasn't it?'

'Oh yes, I freely admit it was. Yes, there's no doubt that your feminine intuition truly is a wonderful and astounding thing. I also admit that probably I was more easily taken in by his deception by the fact of him being a good, keen fellow salmon fisherman.'

Anne now said, 'Poor wee Jeannie was also completely taken in by Daniel. I think perhaps the emotional shock she received at suddenly learning in such a drastic way that he was a vile deceiving traitor rather than quite a friend, was even worse than the stunning physical shock inflicted on her.'

'Ah well, I suppose that's all part of the good wee lass growing up, isn't it?' Ian grinned, 'Of her discovering that not everyone is as good and straightforward as you and I are, Anne. She might have to learn to practise some deception herself if any of Daniel's 'brothers come here to see the river where he drowned and ask not only us, but the hotel staff about his drowning.'

'Yes, I'll need to further instruct her about that possibility, although if all goes as she's hoping she won't be here much longer. She has already volunteered to join the A.T.S. (the female section of the British Army) as soon as she is old enough. It's her ambition to show she can do her bit for Britain almost as well as her two brave older brothers are doing.'

'Oh well, once she's in the A.T.S. she'll learn that in this war the Allies try to gain advantage over the German enemy by using many misleading deceptions.'

'Yes, that's true. Yes, no doubt the innocent lass will get her eyes opened by many amazing things.'

Epilogue

1953

The wearisome restrictions of the austere rationing of food, clothes and petrol that had lingered on into the drab post-war lean years were now, thankfully, things of the past.

Were things to forget in what, hopefully, would be the much brighter years to come as Britain, having won the war and lost her Empire, took her proud, though lesser, place in the United Nations Bright New World.

Thoughts such as these were randomly scattered in the back of Ian Gray's untroubled mind as he drove his pre-war Rover car into his Glen Hotel's attractive grounds.

After parking near its garage he gently patted the dark blue saloon car that, as if as happy as him, purred its gentle contentment as its engine cooled down.

Surely, like Ian, that grand old Rover remembered the almost six long, dreary dismal war years when, denied petrol, it had slept in its garage, ever out of sight, never quite out of mind.

Now when Britain's old familiar foods were again now easily obtainable they were being challenged by the quaint new delicatessens that were mushrooming up from out of Britain's post-war uncertainties. Tempting foreign foods were gradually winning-over reluctant British palates.

Our never very formidable Wop enemies were forgiven their errors as their Chianti gained a favoured place in Britain's re-educated taste.

We even almost forgot the Froggies shameful 1940's surrender as their Sauterne found its way down wary, but getting wine wiser, British throats.

These changes in the Nation's taste were even finding their way to rural Perthshire. They were more and more being felt in the kitchens and wine cellars of Pitlochry's many hotels that were all aglow with fresh paint and other post-war renovations.

As he strolled round to the front of his hotel Ian's contented mood was made even brighter by June's smiling sunshine. This bee-buzzing brightness glowed the massed display of roses that had regained their rightful place of honour after having been ruthlessly displaced by dull, but patriotic wartime vegetables.

The shimmering light and gentle breeze played with the vivid reds, blushing pinks and charming yellows and these roses became things of aesthetic delight while their mingled perfumes were almost overwhelming with a blatant suggestion of sensual pleasures.

The sunshine also gaily sparkled the calm waters of a large loch in front of the hotel. While these roses had regained their pre-war place, this fine loch was something entirely new.

Ian stood enjoying the sun's welcome warmth and drank in the roses alluring scents while he allowed his gaze to wander over that loch, and once again wonder at it being there at all.

It had not been here in his pre-war years. It had only come into being after the quite recent end of the Second World War. So for eyes like his that clearly remembered the old view from the front of the hotel, that loch was something quite unique, something that almost seemed a gross abnormality.

Ian's attention was drawn to someone who also seemed enthralled by this strange new view.

This approaching man pointed at the loch and gave a loud and cheery shout, 'I knew about this. I expected it. But never the less it does seem real strange. It takes some getting used to, doesn't it?'

'Yes, it certainly does,' Ian agreed.

Reaching Ian, this man held out his right hand, 'It's grand to see you again, Mr. Gray.'

As they shook hands, Ian said, 'And it's nice to meet you, too.' He smiled, 'You are Professor Osborne, aren't you?'

'Yeah, I sure am.' He gave a broad grin, 'Surely I haven't changed all that much, have I?'

'Well, you have put on quite a lot of weight.'

'Yeah, I know. That's what comes from living in the United States for the last ten years. Even during the war when you here in Britain suffered under your drastic rationing of almost everything, we in the good old States had few food shortages at all.' He gave a hearty laugh, 'It's thanks to an abundance of massive, thick, rare-done steaks that I've put on this weight.'

Although he did not say so, Ian saw that the professor had also changed in other ways. His ready laughter was deeper and seemed more genuinely cheery than the shrill nervous laugh he used to have. His hair that had been long and wildly unruly was short and well-trimmed. It was flecked with grey. The Bohemian clothes he used to wear had been replaced with a Harris tweed jacket and smart fawn slacks.

Both men's eyes were again drawn to the fine view of this new loch. The professor repeated, 'Yeah, it sure takes some getting used to.'

'You see it from your chalet too, don't you?'

'I surely do. Where I used to see the kids play-park swings and the cute wee nine-hole golf course, all I see now is this brand-new Loch Faskally drowning these two innocent things. And the poor River Tummel that I also saw from my chalet is also drowned. It has to flow unseen through this brash new loch before eager bursting forth below Pitlochry's new Hydro-Electric Dam.'

Ian laughed, 'Yes, all Pitlochry's hotel owners, including me, strongly protested when we heard the Hydro-Electric Board's drastic plans to build a massive dam and create a large new loch. We feared they would ruin our rather perhaps prim and sedate tourist trade.

'However, as you can see, Professor Osborne, we were overruled. We had to admit that the Hydro Board put up a good case for them bringing electricity to every home in the Highlands. And the British

Board of Trade were also very keen that their many thousands of tons of cement, no longer needed for making gun-emplacements and other wartime uses, were used to make these peacetime Hydro Dams.'

'Gee, Ian, that's a perfect example of Swords into Ploughshares, isn't it? Many must have been employed in making that dam.'

'Yes, a workforce of many thousands was engaged in constructing not only that Pitlochry dam but all the other related dams, tunnels and bridges of the entire Tummel-Garry Hydro-Electric Scheme.'

'Did those thousands of hardy navvies cause much trouble? Did they get into fights? Did they scare away your precious prim and proper tourists?'

'Oh, some tourists stayed away during the peak of the vast construction work, but most of our regular guests came as usual. The only serious fight was when some bloody fool got German-prisoners-of-war from the P.O.W. camp near Bruar to help with clearing the site for the new dam. Many of these German soldiers were unrepentant Nazis and that fool expected them to work in harmony with some Poles who had been soldiers in the Free Polish Army and had been fighting the hated Huns who had invaded, occupied and devastated Poland for six long desperate years.

'These Poles and Germans coming face to face resulted in some from both nations ending up in hospital. In different hospitals, of course.' Ian smiled and said, 'As a postscript to this story I myself have seen the defiant swastikas these fanatic Nazi soldiers carved on trees between the west end of the new dam and Fonab Castle.'

'Gee, Ian, that's an interesting story. In some ways I had seemed out of the war in the prosperous safety and comfort of America.' He paused, he gave a bright grin, 'But really I was deeply involved in helping to decide how the war would end.' He said no more despite Ian's enquiring gaze. Instead he changed the subject, 'Oh I hope you don't mind me calling you Ian, Ian. In the States we were all very informal. We soon

219

used Christian names. I liked this pleasant, friendly, democratic habit.'

Ian laughed, 'Oh of course you can call me Ian. But how should I address you, Professor Osborne?'

'My first name is William, but you have my permission to call me Bill.'

Ian again laughed, 'Oh, thank you, Bill. Yes, I like the American's democratic informality too.' Having noticed that Bill had acquired a slight trace of an American accent and had added some American idioms to his distinctive Scottish voice, Ian asked, 'Are you here on holiday, Bill? Are you returning to the States soon?'

'No, I'm not going back there. At least not to work. I intend to get different work here in Britain. If all goes well I might find employment not only in Scotland, but right here in dear old Pitlochry.'

Again before a puzzled Ian could ask more questions, Bill glanced at his watch and said, 'But before I say more about that I could do with a pre-dinner drink then I'll dine in your fine hotel. Will you join me for a drink, Ian?'

'Thank you. I'd like to, but no, I better not. I've promised to help my wife, Anne, prepare for dinner. We're a bit short-staffed just now. But I tell you what, Bill, I'll enjoy a whisky and a good long blether with you after dinner. It'll be good to catch up with things.'

'Yeah, I sure look forward to that. But won't Anne join us for these post-dinner drinks too?'

'No, not this evening. This is her day for her much loved game of bridge with some of her equally keen *girls*.'

So, content and replete after a substantial and tasty three course dinner, the professor met Ian Gray in his hotel's large, comfortable, bright and airy lounge.

'Let's sit over there,' Ian suggested, pointing to a rather secluded corner. 'We'll leave the places with views over Loch Faskally for the other guests.'

They were soon entrenched in large, deep, comfortable, chintzy-covered armchairs.

Their comfort was greatly enhanced by the glass of that magnificent whisky liqueur, Drambuie, lovingly grasped in one hand while the other hand played happy host to a large Havana cigar.

For Ian these twin treasures brought glorious pleasures he had hardly known since the far-off pre-war years.

Almost as one the two men gave deep contented sighs. 'Ah, this is true living, isn't it?' Bill gasped.

Perhaps that was a rhetorical question, but Ian thought it deserved a reply. 'Aye, it certainly is. After Britain's six long war years of grim shortages and strict rationing and those almost equally grim austere post-war years we're just coming out of, surely to God we're entitled to give ourselves a well-earned post-war and post-austerity special treat, aren't we?'

'Gee, of course you are, Ian. You make me feel a terrible cheat by my escaping from your awful wartime hardships by going to the good old U.S.A. But I can assure you that the life I led in America, while comparatively luxurious, was not devoid of real deep worries and terrible stresses.'

Once again Ian was left eager to hear more as they were distracted by two parties of post-dinner guests arriving and getting settled near the lounge's large windows.

It was instructive to overhear these guests' reactions to the view of the large attractive loch they got from where they sat.

The ones who had never been here before admired Loch Faskally's shimmering beauty and casually accepted it as a thing of Nature, one of Scotland's many natural lochs that had been formed when the glaciers melted at the end of the last Ice Age.

Older regular guests at this hotel did not complain but still found it strange not to see the old familiar view they had known of verdant fields abundantly dotted with lazy bloated cattle and the lush green park that had led the way to where the River Tummel gave tantalizing glimpses of itself where it was coyly tucked away under its grassy banks.

The ones who did complain were the older salmon fishers. They expressed their disgust at the loss of the hotel's fine salmon pools. They hated that new Pitlochry dam even though its grand salmon-ladder allowed returning salmon to continue their hazardous journey to the higher spawning redds.

They were still upset by the cruel emasculation of the Falls of Tummel by that brash new Loch Faskally as it greedily rose and drowned half of these once magnificent falls and relegated them to being the mere Linns of Tummel.

With even greater vehemence they denounced not the cruel drowning, but the merciless draining of that grand wee Perthshire salmon river, The Garry, It was now despoiled to little more than bare dry rocks and pathetic trickles into denuded pools where bemused salmon gasped and died.

Ian withdrew his attention from these hotel guests, took another sip of his glorious Drambuie, another soothing pull at his cigar and smiling asked, 'Wouldn't it be damned ironic if in future years that dam, its fish-ladder and that brash new Loch Faskally became Pitlochry's main tourist attractions after us local hotel owners having so actively protested against them?'

Bill answered with a laugh, 'Yeah, I could well see that coming about. Could see these disliked things filling your hotel's bulging coffers.' He then turned more serious, 'That strange drowning of the Tummel Falls reminds me of another even stranger drowning.'

He glanced around to make sure no other guests were within hearing then whispered, 'Was there ever any trouble about the drowning of that would-be assassin, Bailey?'

Also mindful of the need for secrecy, Ian lowered his voice, 'No, that drowning all went smoothly. We had a visit from one of Daniel Bailey's brothers, a sergeant in the British Army. He was keen to see the river where his brother died, so I took him to the pool where his drowned brother was found. He scattered some of his brother's ashes there.'

'He had no suspicions there was anything not quite right about his brother's death?'

'No, none whatsoever.' Ian now looked around to confirm no guests were near. 'No, that shooting dead of Daniel Bailey is a thing known only to us few involved with it.'

'And to those Special Branch detectives from Glasgow.'

Ian nodded, 'Aye that's true. I know my friend, Inspector John Grant, has never heard any more about this secret death from anyone in Special Branch. So, hopefully, this is something that's now quite forgotten.'

Both men raised their Drambuies and drank a silent toast to this secret remaining forever secret.

There was some companionable contented silence while they smoked and drank. Then as he gently tapped off the long grey ash that had been tenaciously clinging to his large cigar Ian grinned, 'Ah good auld Winston was wise to so love his grand Havana cigars. They're far greater than even the best of fags.'

Bill slowly exhaled another cloud of quiet contentment as he wholeheartedly agreed, 'Yeah, old Churchill sure was wise.'

He laughed and gasped, 'Yeah, Ian, cigars are much safer, especially in the United States. I found that fags could be quite dangerous over there.'

'Oh, how was that?'

'I learned my fag lesson soon after I arrived in America in 1943. I shared a railway carriage with a couple of U.S Navy sailors. I got out my cigarettes and before lighting up, offered them to the young Americans, saying "Do you fancy a fag?"

'Their reaction was amazing. Anger flared their faces. Their hands tensed into threatening fists. One sailor demanded, 'What do ya think we are? Damn homos?

'What...What?' I stammered, 'I only offered you a fag! I'm sorry if you Americans don't like British cigarettes.'

'Your cigarettes?" The other asked. 'Is that what yar on about?'

'Yes, of course. I was offering you a cigarette, a fag.'

'A fag? Is that what you Limeys call your cigarettes?'

'Yes, it is. It's a slang name for them.'

'The two sailors burst into helpless laughter. Eventually they stammered, "Gee, we're sorry for our anger. Here in the States a 'fag' means something really different. A 'fag' is a homosexual. Ya understand now, sir?'

'I did. I joined in their renewed loud laughter.'

Ian's laughter now joined with Bill's. They again drank, again smoked. They felt that life was very pleasant. Then Bill said, 'Pitlochry's grand new dam and bright new loch sure take some getting used to. I still find them very strange. In stark contrast to those brand-new things, I regret the loss of Pitlochry's oldest historic building – The Prince Charlie House. When, and why, was it demolished?'

'Oh, it was knocked down in 1947. The way it jutted out into the main road which is part of the A9 highway made it a real hazard to the impatient speeding post-war traffic.'

'Oh, I see. What about that attractive Butter Memorial Fountain? It juts out too, is there any danger of it also being demolished?'

'Oh, I don't think so.' Ian grinned, 'Some very influential local lairds (no names, no pack-drill, as we all used to say in the army) should ensure it remains proudly jutting in its present prominent position.'

'Oh, I see,' Bill repeated then added, 'I also noted another new thing. Something very sad. Those sixteen names neat embossed on Pitlochry's War Memorial in memory of those local men killed in the Second World War.'

'Yes, very sad indeed. Another layer of grief laid on top of that much larger record of grief from the First World War.'

'Yes Ian, I counted more than eighty names from your generation's war.' After a thoughtful pause he said, 'And all those names, and the many millions more, all To The Glory of God, as is almost proudly claimed at the top of that memorial.'

Ian gave a solemn nod, 'Yes, I agree. It's extremely difficult to reconcile all those terrible deaths with a Glorious God.'

It was Bill's turn to nod agreement, 'Yes, perhaps it was an obscure Pagan Fate that decided which young soldiers lived, which died. Surely there's no end to the cruel tricks a Blind Fate inflicts on us poor humans.'

'Aye, that's true,' Ian said, 'and one of the cruellest tricks I know of was not the obvious awful cruelty of sudden unexpected death or the savage ravish of years of pain-filled lingering illness. No, this was a more subtle and cruel ever present menace of death... not of your own death – that would be more easily bearable – but of your only son; your deeply loved only child's death. The poor victim of this stealthy cruelty was a young Pitlochry woman. She had suffered enough in the First World War. Little more than one year after she'd been a lovely young bride she'd become a heart-broken grieving young widow. Her handsome young soldier husband had died in the Flanders mud after having seen their bonnie baby son only one time when he was home on leave. It was only that young mother's devoted love for her baby son that got her through these first black years of grief. Passing time slowly brought her some relief. The love of her strong growing son brought much more. All too soon he grew to handsome young manhood. Then that mother saw with dread her son clad in army khaki and Black Watch tartan just as his father had been little more than twenty years before. This cruel Blind Fate allowed that Scottish widow's only son to survive unharmed through the horrors and dangers of Dunkirk, the North Africa campaigns, the amphibious landings in Sicily and at Anzio and then the long and bloody battles up the length of Italy. Then as the end of the war got ever nearer that increasingly anxious mother and her war-weary son (still quite young in actual years, a Methuselah in battle experience) though separate in body, were joined in mind as both prayed that his great good luck would last, he would survive, still unharmed, until at long, long last this terrible war ended. But this was not to be.

On the very last day of the European war, when Britain was on the brink of rejoicing, the thing that mother had feared for six long war years finally happened, a telegraph-boy tearfully delivered that dreaded telegram: The War Office deeply regrets to inform you... her son, Killed in Action!

That desolate mother could give no coherent reply to this tragic blow of Fate; this long- dreaded awful message cruelly received on the very eve of Peace. Friends, relations, doctor and minister all did their utmost to help her through her darkest tragic grief. But all to no avail.

Only Death could bring her true relief. Her drowned body was found in that very pool on the River Tummel where that traitor Daniel Bailey's drowned body was also officially found.'

'A very cruel and sad trick of Fate indeed,' Bill said. Then after some solemn thoughtful silence he rather apprehensively asked, 'Your son fought in North Africa and Italy too, didn't he? I hope he survived all right.'

'Aye, thank God he did. Yes, Andy came through unscathed.' He said no more, but clearly remembered Andy's post-war confidential, whisky-induced, almost shame-faced admission that as, after six long, brutal, bloody years, the war drew near its longed for end, he and many other battle-weary veterans became increasingly reluctant to take any uncalled for risks. They tried to keep their heads well down. After having seen many good comrades cruelly die or be savagely maimed, they dreaded that that would be the fate in wait for them just as the war ended.'

Ian smiled as he now mentioned brighter things, 'Andy's now managing a Perthshire hotel. He's keen to take over this hotel when Anne and I retire.'

'And how about your two daughters? I hope they came through the war all right too.'

'Oh yes they did. They're both fine. Jane married a Sassenach R.A.F. officer when she was in the W.A.A.F's. They're living with their two bairns down in darkest England. Mary's still a nurse. She's working locally at the P.R.I. (Perth Royal Infirmary).'

After giving this information, Ian thought the time was overdue for Bill – or rather him as Professor William Osborne – to reveal something of the secret scientific war-work he'd been engaged in both here and in America. It must surely have been something of vital importance for the Germans to try to end his secret research by killing him.

Ian knew that, though eight years had passed since the war's end, many of the restrictions of the Official Secrets Act still applied to many things that happened in that war, and this act still cloaked its smothering silence over some things happening in this brave new post-war world's uneasy peace. So perhaps the professor would have to be rather circumspect in what he revealed.

But when Ian somewhat hesitantly requested some enlightenment about his wartime work the professor was quite outgoing. He almost gushed a flood of revealed secrets. He seemed relieved to ease the heavy weight of his dark wartime knowledge by sharing it with a good, non-scientific friend.

He answered Ian's questioning with a question of his own, 'Does the Manhattan Project mean anything to you?'

'No, it doesn't. Should it?'

'No, I suppose it shouldn't. Not many know about that top-secret project. The spark that ignited it was struck by that fantastic genius, Professor Albert Einstein, who in October, 1939 secretly warned President Roosevelt that the Germans might be working towards getting an Atomic Bomb.

'Einstein greatly feared that the nightmare of Hitler possessing Atomic Bombs might become a horrid reality in the not too distant future. So the Manhattan Project came into being. That was code name for the ultra-secret development of America's Atomic Bombs. That was the vital secret scientific work I was engaged in both here, to a limited extent, then in the all-out effort in America.

'We had to win the urgent race to make an Atomic Bomb before the Germans did!'

Ian shook his head as if in disbelief, 'This is all new to me. Oh, I remember you vaguely hinted at fantastic new war-winning secret weapons that time in your Pitlochry chalet after your would-be assassin, Daniel Bailey, was shot dead. I didn't know if I should take you seriously or if it had been merely your generous Glenlivet Malt Whisky talking. Anyway I'd never heard of such things as atomic bombs until one was dropped on Hiroshima then another on Nagasaki.'

'Yes, and even after Nagasaki many Japanese generals still wanted to fight on.'

'Oh, but the total destruction of these cities was terrible, wasn't it?'

'Oh, of course it was. But if there hadn't been these atomic bombs and the allies had had to invade the Japanese mainland, the resulting deaths of allied servicemen could have been over one million! The loss of Japanese military and civilians might have been well over five million.'

'So the use of our atomic bombs was fully justified, wasn't it?'

Ian nodded his agreement, 'Yes, it was. I remember my friend, Inspector John Grant's son, Jamie, saying the same as you, Bill. He had served in a Royal Navy aircraft carrier in the Far East. He had come under suicidal Kamikaze attacks by Jap planes.

He said that all the Allied sailors wildly rejoiced when the atomic bombs ended the war.

'They knew that every Jap commander of P.O.W. camps had been ordered to massacre every one of the Allied Prisoners-of-War held there as soon as the Allies dared invade the sacred soil of Japan.'

Professor Osborne now revealed another secret, 'Oh and one more thing that's known only to those few like me who were in at the heart of things, was that on the morning of the 9th August, 1945, the very day the Nagasaki atomic bomb was dropped, the Japs themselves carried out a test of a small nuclear device near a small island off the Hungnam Coast in the Sea of Japan. Their mini-device only contained about five kilos of uranium. However it was powerful enough to vaporise not only the boat it was on, but also the fishing boats with their Japanese guinea-pig crews moored around it.'

Ian was astounded. He gasped, 'So that race to be first to develop an atomic bomb had actually been a three-way race?'

'Yes, it had. Oh but we were pretty sure the Japs were many years behind us in that desperate endeavour. But the German threat had been another matter entirely.'

'Oh but surely to God there had been no real danger of them getting an atomic bomb before us?'

The professor laughed, 'Oh, it's easy to be sure of that now, but I assure you that for the few of us "in the know" the possibility of that happening was a constant nightmare.

'Yes, for all working at America's top-secret scientific facility at Los Alamos hidden away in New Mexico's vast desert, from our brilliant, inspiring leader, top-physicist Professor Robert Oppenheimer (who became known as *The Father of the Atomic Bomb*) to the humblest junior scientist, the thought that the Germans might get an atomic bomb before us was a nightmare that disturbed our sleep and stressed our daytime minds.

'For Professor Oppenheimer and all the many other German Jews in his team who had got out of Germany before Hitler consolidated his iron grip on power, this nightmare was made much worse by their first-hand knowledge of how many top-class physicists remained in Germany and were working all out on the German war effort. This inside knowledge was truly daunting. Yes, I assure you, Ian, there was a real palpable fear that these proud Aryan Nazi scientists would perform a scientific miracle and present Hitler with the war-winning gift of an atomic bomb long before our Manhattan Project delivered the goods.'

Professor Osborne paused to let that terrifying thought sink into Ian's bemused mind. He then continued, 'Yes, for Churchill, Roosevelt and all us 'in the know' there was a real fear that what Hitler's scientists planned would come about: A German atomic bomb would explode over the heart of London, over Stalin's Kremlin and over either Washington or New York's crammed skyscrapers. The slow progress of our Manhattan Project could result in the real Manhattan becoming a huge radio-active waste of utter desolation.'

The professor again paused then revealed further wartime secrets: The fact that Churchill had had extra secrets worries that his Intelligence Services, having let him down twice, might inadvertently mislead him a third time, and that third error would be a far, far more terrible 'crime.'

'Churchill knew that Hitler was developing new types of weapons. These V for vengeance weapons would bring death and destruction to London. They would avenge the deaths and destruction R.A.F. bombs were inflicting on many German cities.

'The V1 was a jet propelled flying-bomb which top Intelligence Officers assured Churchill would not be ready for use until about two years' time.

'Then out of the blue the first flying-bombs flew their straight steady course for London and inflicted their savage vengeful retribution. Then Churchill was warned that Hitler's new V2 rockets would be a much greater danger as, flying at supersonic speed, we had no defence against them. But again he was assured they would not come into service for at least two years.

'Then from high in a cloudless sky, unseen and unheard until its deafening sonic boom, Hitler's vengeful first V2 rocket exploded near the heart of Whitehall. It was the prelude to a deadly rain of supersonic horror against defenceless war-weary Londoners.

'So, having got their predictions about the V1 and V2 weapons so wrong might these same Intelligence Experts also be far out when they assured Churchill that Hitler's V3 weapon, which they feared might be an atomic bomb, must be at least over two and a half years from being ready for use? Little wonder that this all too likely nightmare of them getting things wrong again made Churchill urge President Roosevelt to do all he could to hurry the Manhattan Project to early success.'

Professor Osborne gave a bright grin (in which Ian thought he could detect a touch of justifiable modest pride) as he triumphantly stated, 'Which, under Professor Oppenheimer's inspiring leadership, of course we did.'

'Oh, Bill, I can sympathise with poor old Winston. Even in my war of 1914/18 we infantry soldiers soon discovered how unreliable army intelligence reports could be. It became a regimental joke that if we saw a soldier Pushing at an office door marked Pull, he must be in the Army Intelligence Corps.'

Ian gave a reminiscent chuckle, 'Then in our more recent World War that old joke amused a much larger audience as it became a regular item in Tommy Handley's glorious, morale-boosting weekly B.B.C. comic wireless show, Itma. For a time a funny ditty was sung about Intelligence Corp soldiers: Pushing at doors marked Pull! Yes, sometimes these supposedly very intelligent Intelligence soldiers (including many officers) could seem very dim.'

Bill laughed, then with a gentle touch of self-mockery admitted, 'Yes, I know from personal experience how many brilliant intellectual minds are quite helpless when it comes to practical every-day things.'

'A case of mind over matter, eh?' Ian suggested.

'Or for us nuclear physicists a case of minds delving into the very heart of Nature's elementary matter. Compared to that most other things can seem very petty.'

Ian nodded his understanding. He knew his un-scientific mind could never enter the professor's astounding world of atoms, neutrons, fusion and fission, so he raised his glass and sipped a silent toast to the much simpler and much more rewarding magic alchemy that had produced this golden, glowing Drambuie liqueur whisky.

For some moments both men sat in thoughtful silence, then Ian asked, 'So Daniel Bailey's attempt to kill you was a small part of that desperate race to be first to produce an atomic bomb? By killing you and no doubt other British and American scientists, the Germans hoped to get ahead in that race?'

'Yes, exactly. Oh and I know that Britain's S.O.E (Special Operations Executive) likewise tried to kill German scientists.' Bill gave an ironic grin, 'When our S.O.E. agents succeeded they were hailed as great brave heroes by the few who knew that was going on.

'When the German agents tried we regarded them as despicable treacherous Nazi scum.'

'Like that awful traitor, Daniel Bailey?'

'Yes, exactly,' Bill repeated. 'You must have found it hard to believe just how deceptive he'd been all the time he'd worked at your hotel while waiting for me to visit my Pitlochry chalet.'

'Yes, I was completely taken in by him.' Ian grinned, 'Even after the Special Branch warning to be wary of him I never thought that such a keen expert fellow salmon fisherman as him could be such a dangerous despicable traitor.'

Bill nodded his agreement, 'Oh, I too know how easy it is to be deceived by people you knew well. This happened to me at the Los Alamos atomic establishment when the Rosenberg husband and wife team were discovered to be committed communists who'd been sending secrets of our Hydrogen Bomb to the Soviets.'

'Oh, they were the ones all the fuss and protests were about earlier this year when they were executed, weren't they?'

'Yes, they were. The husband Julius, was executed in an American prison's electric chair, then the equally guilty wife, Ethel, was killed in the same chair a little while later. This happened in June this year, 1953.'

'You had known them well?' Ian asked.

'Yes, very well. Oh, we all knew they were real left-wingers, but we never thought they'd so betray the United States, the country that gave them freedom when they, German Jews, escaped from the tightening Nazi grip on their country. Yes, it was terrible that after finding refuge from Hitler's vile tyranny they should be so taken in by that other vile tyrant, Stalin.'

Professor Osborne paused then solemnly said 'Oh, many of us scientists at Los Alamos, including our great leader, Professor Oppenheimer, had grave doubts about going ahead with making a Hydrogen Bomb. We could make an accurate guess at what an absolute disaster its radio-active fall-out would be not only for humans alive now, but for generations to come.

'If we made one, the Soviets would in due course also make one. Then between us we'd make even bigger and even more devastating Hydrogen Bombs, ones so huge they'd need an exploding atomic bomb to merely be the trigger to set them off. They would be thousands of times larger and more devastating than anything that had gone before!'

The professor again paused then gave a deep sigh, 'However we were persuaded by our government to do our duty, do the right thing. So last November (1952) we exploded the world's first monstrous Hydrogen Bomb.'

Ian felt compassion for Bill's troubled mind. With gentle empathy he asked, 'So you've decided to give up working on any more of these terrible monsters?'

'Yes, I have. I'm giving up nuclear physics. I've come to live back here in Scotland in my grand Pitlochry chalet.'

'Oh, Bill, surely you're too young to retire? What will you do here?'

The professor smiled, 'Oh, I'm going back to school!'

'To school? You're going to take up teaching?'

'No, I'm going to learn new scientific skills at Edinburgh University. Then I hope to be employed on conservation work on salmon, sea-trout and brown-trout at a new freshwater research establishment that's being set up "somewhere in Perthshire". I've heard it might be established right near here by the shore of this brand-new Loch Faskally.'

'Oh, that would be great,' Ian enthused. 'You getting away from making atomic and hydrogen bombs and helping to conserve our wild Scottish salmon instead would be another perfect instance of swords into ploughshares wouldn't it?'

Bill gave a bright grin, 'Aye, it would. It certainly would. Let's drink a toast to that.'

They raised their glasses and drained the last of their Drambuie.

Both men sat back and gave gentle contented sighs.

After a pleasant silent pause Bill said, 'Oh, another thing I also look forward to once I'm settled here is Pitlochry's other marvellous new post-war arrival: its brand-new Festival Theatre enclosed in its double tents set in the very heart of the town. It's great that they will bring many varied plays to this place.'

Some months have passed. Autumn has draped its bonnie plaid over North Perthshire's tree-blessed landscape.

With blood-red berries and arterial leaves rowans once again flamboyantly flaunt their shameless seduction of besotted blackbirds. Birch and larch compete with one another to put on the most glorious golden glow. Stately oaks display their more mature and un-ostentatious bronze and russet.

Infant Loch Faskally, not yet quite a full three years old, borrowed these seductive trees and gaily painted their vivid reflections on her naked surface while the benevolent October sun slanted down from a cloudless sky. With land and water so well blended it was hard to tell where the one began, the other ended.

The Glen Hotel's grand post-war rose beds were now a routed army; tattered remnants of their mid-summer glory. A few brave blooms put on a defiant show; seemed to compete to gain the unique title of The Last Rose of Summer

Three men, all white-haired, all getting ever more solid and bulky, stood looking out of the hotel's large, west-facing lounge windows. Each man held a post-lunch dram in one hand and a cigarette in the other. As they gazed at the autumnal beauty spread out before them each, to a greater or lesser degree, was touched with aesthetic pleasure.

Ian Gray, the owner of this fine hotel, was the first to speak, 'That bonnie Loch Faskally fair enhances the view from here, doesn't it?'

His old friend John Grant, the ex-police inspector, grinned his reply, 'Aye, it does. It sure does. But you and all your fellow Pitlochry hotel owners did all you could to stop that Hydro-Electric Dam and this attractive loch coming about, didn't you?'

Ian gave a somewhat shamefaced laugh, 'Aye, we did. Yes, John, I freely admit it, I and these others got it completely wrong. Now this view of that glorious loch is one of the first things our new guests enthuse about to Anne and me.'

The third man standing more or less entranced by this autumnal view was another old friend, ex-police sergeant Ewan MacLeod. He, like the police inspector, had been retired for a second time after having returned to wartime police duty. Both felt sure this second retirement would be their last, unless, as they sometimes joked with gallows humour, yet another war broke out and thrust them back into their mothballed uniforms.

Likewise Ian's Home Guard major's uniform was kept neatly pressed and well protected by the distinctive camphor smell of mothballs. But surely it too was unlikely to be needed again. Surely no evil foreign foe was ever going to threaten to invade Great Britain again.

After taking another gulp of his whisky and another draw at his cigarette, Ewan said, 'Och but this new loch view o' those reflected autumn trees is real bonnie aye, and it's real braw tae see that already some o' the ugly scars around the new dam are being cloaked over by fresh grasses, thrusting shrubs an' self-sown wee trees.'

His two companions nodded their agreement. Then all three were distracted from the appealing view by an unusual sound. As one they turned and sent their questing gaze to a cosy corner of the hotel's large lounge.

Again as one they smiled. Ewan MacLeod's smile was especially wide and bright. His face flamed in a flash of delight. His heart thudded with thankful pleasure as for the first time in the last long, sad, ten years he saw and heard his wife, Dorothy, making a brave attempt to laugh. Her welcome sounds were not loud or brash; there was no outright whole-hearted laughter – that was hardly to be expected. Her subdued laughter rippled out as if from gentle stream quiet flowing and grateful merging with the kind laughter of her understanding friends, Anne Gray and Betty Grant.

These two old friends, Ian's and John's wives, had with true deep sympathy and unfailing kindness helped Dorothy get through the long grim years since 1943 when her only son, Colin, had been killed by the Japanese in Burma.

Guided by their deep feminine empathy, Betty and Anne well knew what Dorothy had gone through since the death of Colin. For six long war years they lived with the constant fear that they too, sooner or later, would receive that dreaded official telegram informing them that their son had been killed in action.

While deeply thankful that their sons, one in the Army, one in the Royal Navy, had survived unscathed, still these sensitive mothers truly felt for Dorothy's long-lasting grief. Like Ewan, they were delighted to see her smile and manage at long last to find some relief in a little gentle laughter.

This was what Anne had dared hope for when she'd planned this special lunch-time effort today. She'd instructed her husband, Ian, to leave the three wives in peace to drink their post-lunch coffee by themselves. She'd placed her best silver coffee set to make a brave display on the small table between the three comfortable chintzy armchairs awaiting the three post-lunch wives.

Although the war had been over for eight years the wartime rationing and awful shortages had continued long into the grim austere post-war years, so the full, hot silver coffee pot, the almost overflowing silver cream jug and high heaped silver sugar bowl centred amongst the dainty coffee cups and saucers seemed a welcome promise of the more pleasant and prosperous years to come.

Once the three ladies got themselves settled in the seductive comfort of the large deep armchairs Anne had commenced her happy role of attentive hostess.

The poured coffee gave its delightful aroma, the thick cream sensuously flowed, the genteel silver tongs lifted the cute cubes of brown sugar.

As she sat back and sipped her perfect coffee Anne gave a contented sigh. Betty's and Dorothy's sighs echoed her contentment.

Anne now gave a bright grin, 'Oh isn't this well blended fresh ground coffee absolute bliss compared to the dreary mud-dull Dandelion Coffee we endured without cream or sugar for damned near six long war years?'

'Yes,' Betty smiled and agreed, 'yon awful Dandelion Coffee sure lived up to its more common slang name of Devil's Pish!'

Betty and Anne were delighted when Dorothy smiled, gently laughed, then said, 'Yes, I remember us wee girls thought we were being very naughty when we whispered to each other that these wild dandelion weeds were called *Pee The Beds*!'

Anne and Betty exchanged happy congratulatory glances at this proof that Dorothy could once again smile and quietly and unsurely laugh. They had already noted that she was no longer clad in the funereal blacks she had worn through her first terrible darkest years of grief. She now mainly wore less sombre greys.

Ian and John also exchanged understanding glances. They too were happy to see and hear poor Dorothy's smiles and laughter. Then they met Ewan's eye and with silent empathy expressed their delight at his delight at his wife seeming to regain a much brighter grip on life.

Then again as one, the three men turned, again gazed out over the fine autumnal view of Loch Faskally. In happy unison they drank their drams and smoked their fags.

Even these mere males felt constrained by a strong intuitive instinct that told them there was no need for any words to express what they were all deeply feeling. So they stood in companionable emotion-subdued silence for a short time.

Then, as if hardly knowing what he was saying, Ewan murmured, 'Thank you, John. Thank you, Ian.'

They nodded their silent understanding. They both correctly guessed at what inner turmoil Ewan had suffered while wearing his shield of convincing stoic strength. His hidden grief for the death of his only son must have been as deep and searing as that of his wife's more openly worn grief.

During the war Ewan had his police duties to help distract his grieving mind, but now in the vast leisure of peacetime retirement there was all too much time for his over-active thoughts to dwell on his dead son's all too brief life and his all too cruel death so far away from his loved Scottish Homeland.

True to the spirit of their deep, but unspoken compassion, Ian and John had made a point of always including Ewan in their enjoyable golfing and fishing outings. Although as the years passed and ever increased their cruel arthritic grip on knees and hips while the hills of Pitlochry's grand golf course grew ever steeper, they had to give up their golf for the less strenuous sport of salmon and trout fishing.

Ian now remarked, 'Oh, that new loch's real bonnie, but it's a damned shame it swallowed up my hotel's three salmon pools on the drowned River Tummel.'

John, the ex-police inspector, replied, 'Och, Ian, I think it just as well that the pool where that traitor, Daniel Bailey, was officially drowned has itself been drowned by this new Loch Faskally. We're less likely to have any more of his relations coming to see where he died and possibly sniffing around too much.'

Ian and Ewan nodded their agreement. Then Ewan said, 'No, it would never do for his brothers to ever discover that he'd died not by accidental drowning but by being shot dead by me, a Scottish Police Sergeant.'

'Yes, that would be a real disaster,' John agreed. 'It's what Special Branch feared, knowing it could stir up violent Irish reactions.' He then gave a glimpse of a grin, 'We know the wisdom of letting sleeping dogs lie, don't we? Well it's just as wise for us to keep the truth about how Bailey died forever buried deep in profound sleep.'

'Yes, I whole-heartedly agree,' Ewan said. 'That shooting incident ten years ago almost seems something that happened in a vague and distant dream. Surely it's a thing I'm best to forget.' He then grinned, 'Anyway the man I shot dead all these years ago was not really Bailey – he was an evil wee cowering Jap!'

John and Ian gave understanding laughs. They were delighted that Ewan could now joke about this killing incident. Each time he'd squeezed his revolver's eager trigger he'd avenged the cruel killing of his son by Japanese soldiers. Ian now remarked 'That death of Bailey, or of that Jap, was only one violent death in that terrible war that claimed the lives of millions.'

'Of tens of millions, actually,' John corrected then added, 'Now that Auld Sandy Robertson is also dead there's no longer any fear of him blurting out the truth about Bailey's death. Professor Osborne is the only other one who knows the truth about all this, but, like us, he's signed the Official Secrets Act so he too will keep silent. Oh I think we can be sure our sleeping dog will lie in deep peace. I suppose us few who know the truth should think of this as *Pitlochry's Secret War*, shouldn't we?'

'Yes, and this cover up of this killing must be only one of many unsavoury wartime incidents that are, and might always be, kept profound secrets,' Ian said.

'Unless such secrets are de-classified and revealed to historians in fifty or a hundred years' time,' John suggested.

As the three elderly men gazed out of the hotel's lounge windows they also tried to gaze into the vague future. They hoped they might continue to enjoy reasonable health and live on for a while yet.

For the present however their three glasses were empty and their cigarettes were now stubbed out butts in a large glass ashtray.

The tempting sensual aroma of fresh coffee drifted over to them. They surrendered to this temptation. 'Shall we see if our dear wives have left us any coffee?' Ian asked.

Their dear wives had not left them coolish coffee, but had acquired a fresh hot pot for them.

Soon these three married couples were comfortably ensconced, were delighting to be supping their refreshing fresh coffees and to be sharing their pleasant talk, wide smiles and eager laughter.

Five of them noted with special pleasure how Dorothy MacLeod now joined in with her re-discovered smiles and gentle laughter.

Ewan MacLeod was stirred by deep emotions as he saw his wife seeming regaining her grip on a happier life. He knew that she, like him, would never forget the harrowing experience of having their only son killed, but surely finding stoic strength to get over such human disasters after many years of awful dark grief was the wisest way to go. True to his austere Highland ancestry he gave no outward sign of the deep emotions in his soul. He would never display anything tainted with ugly soppy sentimentality. Instead, his and his wife's re-alive eyes met and expressed their re-alighted love and re-born joy in the promise of better times to come.

There were agreeing smiles all round as Ian lifted his coffee cup and said, 'Let's remember that *Life is Short* and *Death is Final* so lift your cups and drink a toast to us six making the most of our remaining years in quiet wise contentment.'

All toasted the absolute wonder of simply being alive.